# GYMNASTIC KINESIOLOGY

MAVEN BOOKS

# GYMNASTIC KINESIOLOGY

WILLIAM SKARSTROM

Associate Professor of Physical Education

Wellesley College, Wellesley, Mass

MAVEN BOOKS

Chennai　　　　Trichy　　　　New Delhi

MAVEN BOOKS

This edition has been published in india by arrangement with Carson Books, UK

ISBN 978-93-90877-67-6   Maven Books

All rights reserved   No. 44, Nallathambi Street,
Triplicane, Chennai 600 005

MJP 1028   © Publishers, 2023

Publisher :   C. Janarthanan

# Publisher's Note

The legacy of a country is in its varied cultural heritage, historical literature, developments in the field of economy and science. The top nations in the world are competing in the field of science, economy and literature. This vast legacy has to be conserved and documented so that it can be bestowed to the future generation. The knowledge of this legacy is slowly getting perished in the present generation due to lack of documentation.

Keeping this in mind, the concern with retrospective acquiring of rare books has been accented recently by the burgeoning reprint industry. Maven Books is gratified to retrieve the rare collections with a view to bring back those books that were landmarks in their time.

In this effort, a series of rare books would be republished under the banner, "Maven Books". The books in the reprint series have been carefully selected for their contemporary usefulness as well as their historical importance within the intellectual. We reconstruct the book with slight enhancements made for better presentation, without affecting the contents of the original edition.

Most of the works selected for republishing covers a huge range of subjects, from history to anthropology. We believe this reprint edition will be a service to the numerous researchers and practitioners active in this fascinating field. We allow readers to experience the wonder of peering into a scholarly work of the highest order and seminal significance.

MAVEN BOOKS

# PREFACE TO THE SECOND EDITION.

The favorable reception accorded the first edition of the manual was most gratifying. The gradual but steady increase of its use seems to warrant the assumption that it is filling a real want and to justify me in venturing the publication of a second edition.

A number of minor changes in phrasing and construction have been made in an endeavor to make the text clearer. But aside from the correction of a few errors, the addition of three illustrations, and of three titles to the bibliography, no important changes or additions have been made.

*Wellesley College.*

September, 1913.

# PREFACE.

The subject-matter in the following pages appeared, substantially in its present form, in the PHYSICAL EDUCATION REVIEW during 1908 and 1909. This series of articles was planned with a view to present, in a non-technical manner, the application to gymnastics of generally known anatomical facts in conjunction with a few elementary mechanical principles more or less familiar to everyone; and also to correlate such application with certain fundamental conceptions regarding the effect of different uses of the motor organs on their structure as well as on their functional power and control. The larger part of the subject-matter, therefore, is devoted to the analysis of representative types of exercises for the purpose of ascertaining their mechanism and determining, as far as possible, their immediate and permanent effects or tendencies. The aim was to establish in this way a basis for estimating the value or effectiveness of different styles of gymnastic work as regards posture and motor education, and in general to influence gymnastic teaching in the direction of greater definiteness of purpose, choice of material and procedure.

In discussing the mechanism of movements uniformity of conception and execution is assumed. But definitions are sometimes inadequate to insure this in all details, and therefore the mechanism as stated may be at variance with the results of another's observation. In the analysis of the exercises and in attempting to establish certain principles or criteria for their selection and definition, it is not always possible (at present) to prove the points made by scientific demonstration. In many cases, however, this is hardly necessary, careful visual or tactile observation being sufficient to establish the main features. Where this fails or is unreliable, recourse must be had solely to reasoning from a few known facts or from analogy, and the truth or error of such reasoning must be tested by experience. In such cases the conclusions are necessarily tentative. While personal experience or observation makes me feel fairly confident regarding some conclusions or claims made without adducing sufficient proof, I recognize that there is room for difference of opinion and wish to disclaim any assumption of finality of judgment, even if the text at times seems to imply this. My inclination would have led me to wait until more facts could have been established before attempting to write upon this subject. But the scarcity of the literature dealing with it, especially in English, and the lack (at the time these articles were begun) of any work of this kind having a direct bearing on gymnastics, encouraged the hope that even a tentative, elementary treatment might be of some use to teachers and students of physical education.

I take pleasure in acknowledging the kind help given me by Dr. G. L. Meylan in preparing the photographs used for the illustrations and by Mr. A. I. Prettyman in the preparation of some of the line drawings. To Dr. C. J. Enebuske and the Boston Normal School of Gymnastics I shall always be indebted for having my interest in the subject aroused, for receiving my first instruction in it as well as inspiration to further study and observation. This interest has been kept alive and stimulated by profitable discussions with Drs. L. Collin, Theodore Hough, J. H. McCurdy, G. L. Meylan, L. H. Gulick and others. Finally, to the faithful efforts and intelligent questionings of normal students at Chautauqua and Columbia Summer Schools and at Teachers College, I owe the clearing up of many puzzling problems in Gymnastic Kinesiology.

*Columbia University.*

June 1, 1909.

# The Distinctive Features of Gymnastics, as Compared with Dancing, Games and Athletics.

The procedures used as means of physical education may be grouped under the following heads: games and athletics; dancing and gymnastics. The first two are largely objective in their nature, involving bodily action and control with reference to something outside the individual. Such bodily action is usually measured or judged according to results produced on some object, such as a ball, a hammer, the point of a foil, the body of an antagonist; or it may be measured in terms of time or space, either absolutely or as compared with some other individual. In any case, the attention of the performer is fixed, not on himself, but on something outside of himself. His immediate object is to execute movements requiring often skill and delicate adjustment, usually great intensity of effort, or else endurance; and all this, not for the sake of the movements themselves—for their æsthetic, physiological or other effects—but for the sake of obtaining some objective result. His satisfaction consists, for example, in being able to propel himself farther or faster through space than the next man; to elude a pursuer; to place an object where his opponents cannot catch it, as in baseball, handball, etc., or where it will do the greatest amount of execution, as in bowling and boxing. He does not care, at least for the time being, whether such movements are, *per se*, injurious or beneficial, graceful or otherwise, as long as they accomplish his purpose. Instances are not lacking where even life or death did not matter, although the issue was merely friendly rivalry.

Dancing and gymnastics, on the other hand, are largely subjective in character. Here the bodily action and control have reference to the individual himself, to the relation of the parts of his body to each other, and to the immediate or remote æsthetic, physiological or anatomical effects produced by the movements. Hence the movements and positions are made to conform to some arbitrary standard, not readily measured or expressed in terms of time and space, absolute or relative, but judged by the individual himself or the onlooker according to the closeness of conformity to this standard. The latter may be merely an abstract idea based on æsthetic conceptions, or it may be based on anatomical or physiological knowledge. It is the "form," "style," "grace" or whatever term we may use, that counts. The attention is always on the individual himself, or on some accessory which for the time being may be considered a part of himself, such as dress or drapery in dancing; clubs, wands and other paraphernalia in gymnastics. The individual's satisfaction is not dependent on the accomplishment of some result external to himself, but on his ability to move the parts of his body, or his body as a whole, in certain rhythm, through or to certain attitudes or positions, requiring always precision, often speed, occasionally endurance. Sometimes external objects may be involved, as in the case of fixed gymnastic apparatus, but the performer's efforts are not directed toward these; they simply serve as points of support or fulcra to influence his own movements, to increase their scope, difficulty, variety; enabling him to check, increase, or change the direction of his momentum, to distribute the work in varying proportions to different parts of his body, etc.

It is not always easy to draw the line between the two kinds, as many forms of activity involve both of the principles mentioned, or may be made to do so. For example, competitive jumping may be made to include certain details of form or style, such as position of the body while in the air, when landing, or leaving the ground. Similar details may be included in the rules of many games and sports. Again, gymnastics and dancing may be made competitive and so in a sense become objective, but only secondarily. In any such combination of the two elements the primary distinction would always remain.

The effects on the individual of these types of activity are in some respects similar, in other respects not. The differences are of kind, as well as of quality and degree. That this is the case, and of considerable importance, is becoming increasingly recognized, at least by the profession. In the minds of the laity there is still much confusion on this subject, and one kind is usually considered equivalent to another. In such cases the similarities only are perceived, namely the immediate, obvious organic effects of muscular exercise. Where differences are recognized, they are often of an incidental kind, such as the opportunities, or lack of them, for getting fresh air; the element of pleasure or predilection, etc.; or they may be merely popular notions regarding the hygienic, or developmental and "muscle building" power of each.

The general organic effects of muscular exercise are of course common to all kinds of bodily activity, varying in intensity and amount according to the kind, vigor, duration, continuity and distribution of the work. The same is true, in a general way and with the same qualifications, as regards muscular development. In gymnastics, however, we can more readily select the kind, gauge the duration and intensity, and control the localization and distribution of the work, and therefore more effectively determine the character and direction of the development. Here lies, in fact, one of the main differences between the two types. In games and athletics the work is instinctively (and purposely sometimes) done in the easiest way, by many muscular groups, and those the strongest, regardless of postural effects, if only the mechanical conditions can be made more favorable for immediate purposes. Left to the individual's own (or the coach's) selection, as is usually the case, such forms of activity are chosen as are best adapted to his own peculiarities of physique and which therefore promise greatest likelihood of immediate success. Motor and postural habits already acquired thus tend to become more fixed, and the chances for an even, all-around development are diminished. In gymnastics (of the right kind) the conditions are reversed. The efforts are here directed toward equalization of development* and the formation of good habits of movement and carriage. This is accomplished by well-defined, localized movements, in which the weaker muscles are brought into powerful, quick, or sustained action, and a forced erect position is maintained throughout.

Another respect in which the effects of the two types of work differ is in the kind of bodily control cultivated by each. In games and athletics the individual is constantly called upon to meet a variety of situations requiring quick perception and judgment, and demanding muscular efforts of varying intensity and adjustment according to the needs of the moment. The ability to judge quickly and accurately the distance, speed and direction of moving objects and to adjust the muscular efforts relative to these is often a marked feature. The motor control resulting from this kind of work is one which enables the individual to meet special classes of situations: special skill, sometimes very limited in scope, as in a standing broad jump, or in the shot put; sometimes very varied, as in basket ball or boxing. The more numerous and different the games or sports in which the individual engages, the greater becomes his fund of reflex or automatic coördinations, his power of adaptation, in a word, his physical efficiency. Let us for the present call this kind of control *objective*. Its value is obvious and would alone justify the giving of athletics and games a

---

*This term is not intended to apply to minor details of measurement of the two sides of the body, but is used in a more general sense applying to all parts.

prominent place in any comprehensive scheme of physical education. The moral and social training is of course of even greater importance, but that does not come within the scope and purpose of this discussion.

The motor control cultivated by dancing and gymnastics is, like the work, of a subjective kind. It does not directly make the individual more efficient as regards influencing external objects, but it does mean ability to manage himself. It means, among other things, a better sense of equilibrium, increased power of adjustment to situations in which change of base or support are frequent and marked features. It includes, usually, ability to judge and manage his own momentum to best advantage. The posture sense, too, is cultivated, and on this depends, to a great extent, ability to assume and maintain a good carriage. Of course, the proper structural relations and muscular tone are also essential factors in this, but as already suggested, and as will be shown more clearly later, gymnastics are more effective in producing this than is any other kind of work. The ability to make precise, speedy and powerful localized movements, which forms the basis of so many kinds of specialized skill, and which is an important element in all effective and economical action, is demanded and acquired by well-defined, clean-cut, gymnastic exercises. In dancing, some of these elements are present to a greater or less extent. Besides, there is required a nicety in the adjustment of effort, in the shifting and redistribution of the body weight, in the smooth sequence and blending of movements of rhythmical alternation and recurrence, which is bound to increase the power of coördination, to train the sense of rhythm, to eliminate stiffness, jerkiness and awkwardness of movement, and the self-consciousness that is both a cause and an effect, thereby enabling the individual to manage himself to better advantage in the ordinary movements of daily life. This kind of control might be called *subjective.* It is often expressed in such terms as grace, bearing, presence, etc., and is probably of more importance in the social relations of life (and perhaps in business too) than we are apt to think. Much of it is, of course, acquired unconsciously under favorable home and social conditions in early life, but it is safe to say that the need of training in this respect still remains fairly general, and that it is one of the legitimate functions of physical education to meet this need. A cultivation of subjective control is of advantage, also, as a preliminary to, and a basis for, the objective training obtained by a practice of games and athletics. The two should go hand in hand, each supplementing and balancing the other. Perhaps there is no fundamental difference between objective and subjective control, the former being simply the ability to apply the latter in various directions.  Here, as everywhere, it is difficult to draw hard and fast lines.  But those who have had occasion to observe and inquire into the physical characteristics of great numbers of youths and adults cannot have failed to notice the frequent occurrence of cases in which the one or the other type of control seemed to predominate, and the corresponding difference in the kinds of activity which represented the physical training of the individuals.

If it be true, in a general way, that games and athletics are conducive to objective efficiency, gymnastics and dancing to subjective harmony—and I think the experience of teachers of physical education will bear it out—it next becomes of interest to inquire into the effectiveness of particular types of each, the principles underlying selection, methods of procedure, management and teaching which would produce the most rapid and permanent results.  The magnitude of such an inquiry necessitates division of the subject and even limitation to certain topics within each division.  Our study will, therefore, be confined largely to gymnastics, and even in this limited field only certain phases will be discussed in detail, chiefly those of a technical character, relating to the definition and mechanism of movements and positions, and to their correct execution.

Gymnastics, it is generally conceded, constitute one of the most effective means of correcting minor defects of development and faulty structural relations resulting from the unfavorable influences of modern conditions of life.  When applied to growing individuals, this statement might be put in positive form by saying that gymnastics most effectively conduce to normal growth and development.  They counteract the pernicious effects of sedentary, school-desk life, they offset and supplement the unequal and partial activity of daily life as well as of games and athletics.  But the great value of gymnastics, especially when supplemented by dancing, in the cultivation of subjective control, is not so generally appreciated.  Nor are the differences between these two kinds of subjective activity always clearly understood.

Gymnastics and dancing are closely related, fundamentally, and are often combined in varying proportions while being called one or the other.  In dancing the movements are always continuous and rhythmical, they are less localized, less sharply defined than gymnastic movements; they involve blended but partial action of a great number of joints and muscles rather than complete, powerful action of a few.  In gymnastics the movements are usually not continuous, but consist of a series of changes of position, each position being clearly defined and held a varying length of time.  While gymnastics may be rhythmical it is not of advantage to have the rhythm even and uniform.  This tends irresistibly to make the movements lose in vigor and completeness, and therefore in their own distinctive effectiveness. In gymnastics, as in everything else, it is better to aim at powerful and rapid effects in a few directions, rather than partial, mediocre results in many. Gymnastics are specialized, artificial forms of activity, capable of being taught by logical and intensive methods, and of producing satisfactory results in the way of harmonious development, improved posture and increased speed, accuracy and power of motor adjustment. But this cannot be reasonably expected if the exercises constituting the gymnastic lesson do not call for this kind of action, or if they do so nominally, are arranged, combined and taught in such a way as to defeat their own objects, or at least reduce their effectiveness to a minimum. For example, if slow and partial, or very complex movements of one part of the body, say the trunk, are combined with what is intended to be quick, vigorous and complete movements of another part, say the arms and shoulders, the latter will inevitably assume the character of the former, and so amount to very little from any point of view. The greater the complexity of the movements, relative to the ability of the individual or class, the smaller are the chances for effective execution. This will also be the case if all kinds of movements are made to conform to a uniform, even rhythm, and especially if accompanied by soothing, dreamy music, or worse yet, by a featureless, mechanical hammering on a piano. The work then really becomes dancing, but dancing of an inferior grade, such as would be scorned and repudiated by any good teacher of dancing. As gymnastics it has chiefly the value of gentle exercise. When this is the main object sought, such work may be defended, and there are doubtless conditions—aside from classes of small children, where it may be perfectly legitimate—under which no other kind of work would be feasible. This might, for example, be the case with classes of working women, at least to begin with. But such conditions are probably not as numerous, or at least as permanent, as is often supposed. This style of work is, however, apt to please the pupils, at least for a time; and it makes teaching comfortable and easy. It may be compared to methods of teaching children language symbols and elementary numbers by incorporating them in games, songs and rhymes; or to some conceivable method of teaching grammar and arithmetic through forms expressed in terms of poetry and music. Gymnastics of this type lose most of their distinctive features. The movements are done in the easiest manner, are incomplete and vague, usually listless or else oscillatory, i.e., the terminal and intermediate positions are not sufficiently marked. Opportunities for correction by the teacher are thus lost, and the pupils are encour-

aged to form habits of looseness of conception as well as of
execution. Most teachers have had the experience of being told
by a prospective pupil that he or she has had gymnastic training
so and so long, and is quite familiar with the work, while even the
most casual observation of the pupil's motor or postural habits,
and the quality of his subsequent work, seem utterly to contradict
this, or to suggest that the work previously done had been of a
character which failed to produce those effects·which gymnastics
stand for. Analogies to this in other fields are only too numerous,
the most common, perhaps, being language. Again, many people
lose faith in the effectiveness of gymnastics, because they have
found for themselves that years of honest but misdirected efforts
have failed to do for them what they had been led to expect. This
may of course be explained partly by the tendency of some
teachers to make excessive claims for something about which they
have more faith and enthusiasm than detailed knowledge, partly
by popular misconceptions about the whole subject. The latter
was well illustrated recently by the reply of the sporting editor
of a newspaper to a query sent in by a young man regarding the
best way to improve round shoulders. "Join a gym, work hard at
dumbbells, chest weights, rowing machines, boxing and handball."

While it is perfectly legitimate and desirable, whenever feasible,
to give in each gymnastic lesson some work in the nature of
dancing, games or athletics to supplement the gymnastics, it is
well to make each distinct from the other, not only by name and
place in the lesson, but also by the character of the work itself,
and by the method of teaching it. Let the gymnastic exercises
stand out in contrast to the others by being "clean-cut," definite
in type, simple and localized rather than complex and general, or,
if relatively complex, capable of analysis, of being resolved into
simple component parts, each of which is marked or punctuated,
so to speak, by a sharply defined position. And insist, by all the
resources of the art of teaching, on accurate execution of the
movements and on at least a momentary maintenance of the intermediate and terminal positions. Define the exercises in a way
to induce completeness of movement in a small number of joints,
and in directions which are neglected in the ordinary movements of daily life and even in most games and athletics, and in
which, therefore, mobility tends to become diminished. This will
of course mean complete and powerful contraction of the muscles
on that side of the joints. These muscles, because seldom used
in that way, are apt to be deficient in development or tone, or both.
At the same time the opposite structures, muscular and fibrous,
which offer resistance to completeness of movement, will be
subjected to strong tension. Furthermore, the effort to localize
the movement, i.e., to move as much as possible in one place and

as little as possible elsewhere, will bring into tonic or static action many other muscles in order to keep other parts from moving. When "other parts" include the trunk or shoulder blades (and that is very often the case), the muscles responsible for the proper posture of these parts are given valuable training in endurance and control, a training particularly well adapted to their special function, that of support. This is of as much importance as their increase in size and strength, which determines their efficiency as purely motor organs.

A practice of well-defined, localized movements, is, in the long run, conducive to economical motor habits by increasing the individual's power of localized muscular contraction. This implies a saving, not only in the number of muscles needed to produce a given movement, but also of the number needed to prevent movement elsewhere. In other words, the inhibition of movement becomes more and more a central, instead of a peripheral process, a matter of reflex, rather than voluntary attention. In practice this should not occur to any considerable extent, as it is desirable to have the total amount of muscular work as great as possible. It need not occur if the selection and progression of the exercises are such as to make them always sufficiently difficult and severe, no matter how far advanced the pupils may be.

By making the majority of the gymnastic exercises as speedy as is consistent with their nature and mechanism, and by doing at least a part of the work to the word of command, habits of quick and accurate motor response to given situations are formed. These become multiplied and more firmly fixed by application in games and athletics, improving the quality of the latter, and so increasing the gain in objective as well as subjective control.

In gymnastic apparatus work, especially in such exercises as jumping, vaulting, climbing, a kind of subjective control is cultivated which is usually expressed by the term agility. This implies ability to manage the bodily momentum, when on the feet, when suspended on or supported by the arms; or a combination of these. This is a large element in physical efficiency. Gymnastics of this kind are very closely related to athletics, the difference being, as already pointed out, that in corresponding types of athletic competition "the form" (position of body, etc.) is of no special significance, except as it facilitates the performance of a particular feat, whereas in gymnastics it is the principal thing and should never be lost sight of. In gymnastic work of this kind the variety may be made much greater and the progression finer than in athletics. This leads to greater versatility and range of control.

The effectiveness of gymnastics in the directions indicated will then depend on the style of exercises taught, and this in turn on the teacher's conception of the objects of the work, his ideals and standards, and his ability to present it in such a way as to elicit the greatest amount of coöperation from his pupils. As a basis for all this an understanding of the physiological effects and the anatomical mechanism of the exercises is essential. The former will guide him in determining the amount, duration and intensity of the work, the latter in the selection, definition, arrangement and progression of the exercises. Both are needed for an intelligent appreciation of the needs of the individual or class, for a judicious choice of the means, and for a proper estimate of what may be accomplished.

The following chapters will be devoted to a study of the anatomical mechanism of the most common and representative types of gymnastic movements and positions.

# A. UPPER TRUNK AND SHOULDER REGION.

*Importance of trunk movements.*  In the introductory part an effort was made to point out the place of gymnastics in a comprehensive scheme of physical training, and particularly the effectiveness of systematic, well-defined, accurately executed gymnastic movements in equalizing growth and development, and in cultivating that kind of subjective control on which erect carriage, agility and efficient, economical motor habits depend.  Of such gymnastic exercises, the most important are those involving the trunk, shoulder and hip regions.  The relations of the bony and fibrous structures of these parts; the strength, tone, endurance and control of their muscles obtained through the proper and regular exercise of those muscles, determine largely the results we may expect in the directions indicated.  Biologists and psychologists are pretty well agreed on the fundamental character of such trunk movements, and on the importance of their early cultivation in relation to normal growth and development, not only of the osseous and muscular systems of the trunk, but also of the great vital organs contained in it.  Besides, as Tyler has so clearly pointed out, the proper development of the fundamental brain centers, and indirectly of the whole central nervous system, is intimately connected with and dependent on abundant and varied activity, in early life, of the large muscles in these regions.*  During the later stages of the developmental period the continued cultivation of these central and fundamental neuromuscular mechanisms is conducive to a more complex and finer motor control, thus increasing the individual's power of adapting himself to his environment.  This is done by gradually demanding more definiteness, finer "shades" of distinction, more accurate localization, greater variations of speed, etc., in the same trunk, shoulder and hip movements.  In this way new paths of motor associations are opened up, new, or at least clearer, motor ideas are formed, finer motor ideals are established, and a more complete realization of latent possibilities of muscular coördination is attained.  Finally, the purely physiological effects of trunk movements are of primary and equal importance, in the maintenance of health and organic vigor, from childhood to old age.

In discussing the anatomical mechanism of the gymnastic movements no attempt will be made to analyze them with mathematical accuracy, or in terms of mechanics.  The principal aim will be to show how, by apparently small variations of definition

---

*J. M. Tyler, *Growth and Education.*

and execution, the character of the movements may be considerably modified, and their effectiveness enhanced or diminished.

### ANATOMY—I.  JOINTS AND MOVEMENTS.

To begin with, it will perhaps be helpful to review briefly some of the most important anatomical facts having a bearing on the kind and range of movement in the joints of the regions to be considered, and the muscles producing or modifying these movements.

The bony framework of the trunk consists of: (1) the spinal column, forming its main support and sustaining the weight of the head, shoulders and thorax; (2) the thorax, a bony-cartilaginous cage, consisting of the ribs, articulating in front, by their cartilages, with the sternum, and behind, directly, with the thoracic spine; (3) the shoulder girdle, an incomplete bony ring formed by the clavicles and scapulæ, articulating with each other by means of the acromio-clavicular and with the trunk by the sterno-clavicular joints; (4) the pelvis, another bony ring articulating with the lower end of the spine.

The spine as a whole is fairly mobile by means of the intervertebral disks and the joints between the articular processes of the vertebræ. The mobility in the different regions of the spine varies in range and kind. The chief factors which determine this are: (1) the thickness of the intervertebral disks, (2) the plane of the surfaces by which the articular processes meet, and (3) the tightness or laxness of the ligaments, especially of those connecting the articular processes. In the thoracic region the attachment of the ribs to the vertebræ is a very important factor influencing mobility or rather limiting it. Generally speaking, mobility is greatest in the lumbar spine, smallest in the thoraic. As regards the different kinds of movement, flexion, extension and hyperextension are most free in the lumbar region. Here the existing physiological curve is one of hyperextension (including often the twelfth thoracic vertebræ, and sometimes the eleventh). This hyperextension may be carried considerably further. The opposite movement, flexion, is correspondingly free, reaching and passing somewhat beyond the straight line, in the average young person at least. In the thoracic region the spine is normally in a state of flexion. This may be increased a moderate amount. The opposite movement of extension can only be carried to the straight line, and barely that in most persons. The range of flexion and extension is therefore not very great here, chiefly owing to the attachment of the relatively rigid thorax to this part of the spine; also, the intervertebral disks are here thinner and the ligaments tighter than in the other regions, notably

the lumbar.  For these reasons the side-bendings also are here less
free than in the lumbar region.  Rotation, on the contrary, is
much freer in the thoracic (amounting to about 30 degrees each
way) than in the lumbar region, where the locking of the articular
processes prevents all but a very slight amount of this kind of
movement.  The cervical spine is capable of all the movements
enumerated, the freedom and range being intermediate between
the other two.  Rotation is, however, greater here than in the
lumbar spine.

The chest, although relatively rigid as compared with the whole
spine, is yet capable of considerable variations in its diameters.
This is accomplished by: (1) a rolling movement of the posterior
portions of the ribs (directed outward, downward and a little
backward) on an axis passing through the costo-central and costo-
transverse joints; (2) by a twisting and straightening movement
of the rib cartilages; and (3) by a gliding motion in the chondro-
sternal and inter-chondral joints.  On account of their obliquity
and peculiar curves, the resulting movement of the ribs is one
which for convenience of description it is customary to· analyze
into two parts: elevation, involving a raising of the anterior ends
of the ribs and the sternum and a tilting of the latter (due to the
comparative immobility of the first pair of ribs); and eversion,
implying a "spreading out" of the ribs laterally, a moving outward, as well as upward of their convex lower borders.  In this
way both the antero-posterior and transverse diameters of the
chest are increased.  This movement of the ribs, while involving
the complete range of motion in the costo-vertebral joints (and
this is not very great on account of the number and shortness of
the costo-vertebral ligaments) is considerably amplified by the
supplementary movements of the thoracic vertebræ in the direction of extension.  In other words, whenever there is an effort at
extreme chest expansion, the thoracic spine is straightened at the
same time.  Conversely, any movement of the thoracic spine influences the position of the chest, as, aside from the short, tense
ligaments, the intimate muscular connection between the vertebræ and the ribs, will cause the latter to follow any movement of
the former, even before the limit of motion in the costo-vertebral
joints has been reached.

The movements of the shoulder girdle, involving the sterno-
clavicular and acromio-clavicular joints, may be most readily,
though imperfectly, expressed in terms of movement of the
scapula.  Thus (1) elevation' and (2) depression of this bone
imply movement in both of the joints mentioned, of such a nature
as to keep the scapula from being displaced in other directions
than directly upward and downward, and from changing its plane.
Similarly the scapula may be moved away from and toward the

mid-spinal line by complementary movements of the two joints. This is (3) abduction and (4) adduction of the scapula. Finally the scapula may be made to swing around on an approximately central axis, in such manner that the glenoid cavity will face almost directly upward, and the vertebral scapular border will approach the horizontal, with the lower angle close to the posterior axillary line. This is called (5) rotation upward, and the return to the ordinary position (and a little beyond it) (6), rotation downward. While these movements of the scapula are described, for the sake of simplicity as "pure," that is, each occurring without any admixture of any other, this does not occur naturally. Usually two or more are associated. Only by very skillful muscular coördination and considerable effort can pure movements be approximated. All these scapular movements are supplementary to the movements in the shoulder joint, and by means of them the range of movements of the upper arm is nearly doubled.

The shoulder joint proper—between the head of the humerus and the glenoid cavity of the scapula—allows about 90° to 110° of all kinds of motion: flexion and extension, a moving of the arm forward (upward) and return, and also a slight amount of hyperextension, i.e., a moving of the arm backward; abduction and adduction, a moving of the arm directly outward (away from the side) and return, and also a slight amount of hyperadduction when combined with flexion; a combination or rather a succession of these—circumduction; and finally rotation inward and outward of the humerus on its length axis a varying amount (from 30° to 40° each way). These movements are checked and limited by the capsular ligament, the coraco-humeral ligament, by approximation of the tuberosities of the humerus to the arch formed by the acromion and coracoid processes of the scapula and the ligament connecting them; and lastly—though first in point of time—by stretching of the muscles whose tendons surround the joint on all sides and act as accessory ligaments.

### II.  MUSCLES.

The various movements of the spine are produced (aside from the part played by gravity) by muscles, attached by one or both ends to the spine, and also by muscles attached to the chest, shoulder girdle and pelvis. Thus active flexion of the whole spine would be brought about by the anterior neck muscles, the pectorals (the internal intercostals), the straight and oblique abdominal muscles, and, under·some circumstances, by the latissimus dorsi. Active extension and hyperextension would in general be produced by the erector spinæ and its upper prolongations, all the deeper and some of the superficial back muscles, such as serratus posticus superior and inferior, levator anguli scapulæ and trapezius. Active side-bending, or straightening up from the position of side-bending, would involve the front and back muscles of the corresponding side. Rotation or trunk twisting would be produced by consecutive relays of oblique muscles on both sides of the spine and by the external oblique abdominal muscles of one side working in conjunction with the internal oblique of the other side. These will be discussed in more detail in connection with the analysis of gymnastic movements.

The muscles which move the chest are: (1) the muscles of ordinary inspiration—external intercostals (anterior portion of internal intercostals), levatores costarum, scaleni; (2) those of forced inspiration—sterno-mastoid and the anterior neck muscles attached by their lower ends to the sternum, the subclavius, lower (anterior) part of latissimus dorsi, lower serratus magnus, lower pectoralis major, pectoralis minor, serratus posticus superior, accessorius ad ilio-costalem, cervicalis ascendens, and indirectly most of the other back muscles; (3) the muscles of forced expiration—the internal intercostals, the abdominal muscles, quadratus lumborum, serratus posticus inferior, ilio-costalis, longissimus dorsi, infracostales and triangularis sterni. The diaphragm in its descent tends to draw the lower ribs somewhat (upward and) inward. This is resisted by the quadratus lumborum and serratus posticus inferior, which may thus in certain forms of breathing be considered as aids to forced inspiration.

The muscles which move the scapula are as follows:

(1) *Elevators:*
Upper trapezius,
Levator anguli scapulæ,
Rhomboids.

(2) *Depressors.*
Lower trapezius,
Lower serratus magnus,
Pectoralis minor
  and indirectly
Subclavius,
Latissimus dorsi.
Lower pectoralis major.

(3) *Abductors:*
Serratus magnus,
Pectoralis minor
  and indirectly
Pectoralis major.

(4) *Adductors:*
Trapezius,
Rhomboids,
  and indirectly
Latissimus dorsi.

(5) *Rotators upward:*
Trapezius,
Serratus magnus.

(6) *Rotators downward:*
Rhomboids,
Levator anguli scapulæ,
Pectoralis minor
  and indirectly
Latissimus dorsi,
Lower pectoralis major.

The following shoulder joint muscles move the humerus on the scapula, in any position of the latter bone:

(1) *Flexors:*
Pectoralis major,
Anterior deltoid,
(Short head of biceps,
Coraco-brachialis).

(2) *Extensors:*
Latissimus dorsi,
Teres major,
(Long head of triceps).

(3) *Abductors:*
Deltoid,
Supraspinatus,
Long head of biceps.

(4) *Adductors:*
Latissimus dorsi,
Teres major (and minor),
Pectoralis major,
Long head of triceps.

(5) *Rotators inward:*
Subscapularis,
Pectoralis major,
Latissimus dorsi,
Teres major,
Anterior deltoid.

(6) *Rotators outward:*
Infraspinatus,
Teres minor,
Posterior deltoid.

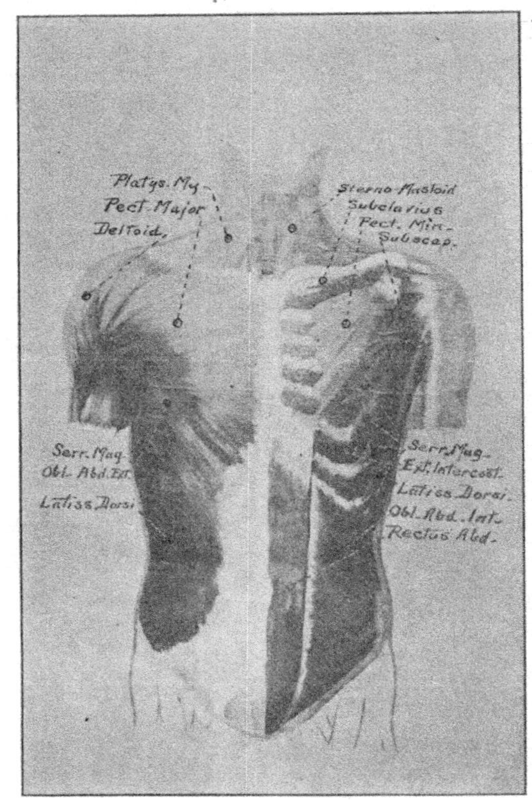
Platys. My
Pect. Major
Deltoid,
Sterno-Mastoid
Subclavius
Pect. Min.
Subscap.
Serr. Mag.
Obl. Abd. Ext.
Latiss. Dorsi
Serr. Mag.
Ext. Intercost.
Latiss. Dorsi.
Obl. Abd. Int.
Rectus Abd.

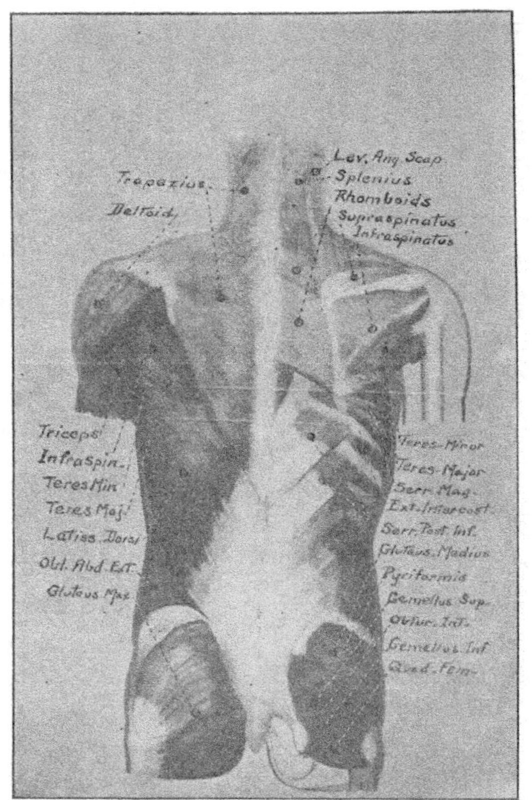
Trapezius.
Deltoid,
Lev. Ang. Scap.
Splenius
Rhomboids
Supraspinatus
Infraspinatus
Triceps
Infraspin.
Teres Min
Teres Maj.
Latiss. Dorsi
Obl. Abd. Ext.
Gluteus Max.
Teres Minor
Teres Major
Serr. Mag.
Ext. Intercost.
Serr. Post. Inf.
Gluteus Medius
Pyriformis
Gemellus Sup.
Obtur. Int.
Gemellus Inf.
Quad. Fem.

It will be noticed that all the muscles which move the scapula and a majority of those which move the humerus on the scapula act in more than one capacity. Thus the trapezius as a whole is both an adductor and a rotator upward of the scapula, while its upper portion elevates and its lower portion depresses this bone (by movement in the sterno-clavicular joint). Similarly the serratus magnus as a whole abducts and rotates the scapula upward, while its lower portion also tends to depress it bodily. The pectoralis minor abducts, depresses and helps to rotate it downward; the rhomboids and levator anguli scapulæ adduct, elevate and rotate it downward. The reasons for this multiplicity of action are found in the extensive lines of origin of most of these muscles on the chest or spine and the relatively small extent of surface of their insertion on the scapula; in the oblique direction of their fibres relative to the movements named; and finally (as regards rotation) in the position of their scapular insertions and the direction of their pull relative to the sterno-clavicular and acromio-clavicular joints.

Among the muscles which produce movement in the shoulder joint we find a few capable of chiefly one kind of action. Such are the supra- and infraspinatus, the subscapularis and perhaps the teres minor. The others act in two or more capacities, as, for example, the pectoralis major, which raises the arm from the fundamental position forward, upward and inward across the chest (a combination of flexion and hyper-adduction), while from any position of the arm above the horizontal it moves it downward and inward across the chest. In conjunction with the deltoid the pectoralis major is therefore a flexor of the shoulder joint while in conjunction with latissimus dorsi it is an adductor. At the same time it also helps in rotation inward. The reasons for the varied actions of the shoulder joint muscles are similar to those given regarding the scapular muscles.

Another point to be noted is the indirect action of the pectoralis major and latissimus dorsi on the scapula. They are not attached to this bone, but nevertheless greatly influence its movements. When the limits of motion in the shoulder joint have been reached and the ligaments are stretched or the bony processes in contact, the two bones (humerus and scapula) are to all intents and purposes one, and the pull of the above named muscles is thereby exerted on the scapula. This happens even before the limits of motion in the shoulder joint have been reached, owing to the intimate muscular connection between the two bones. This is of considerable importance in the definition and execution of gymnastic exercises, and will be referred to again.

From the foregoing it will be seen that rarely, if ever, is any given movement of the scapula or arm produced by one muscle, or even by a single group. Each kind of movement is the result of the combined action of many muscles pulling in divergent lines, acting partly against, and so neutralizing each other, partly in the same direction.

Resultant movement. The exact direction or plane of the movement will depend on the number and obliquity of the muscles involved, and the amount of pull (and leverage) exerted by each. It is in this way that so many "shades" of adjustment are possible.

Before taking up the study of the anatomical mechanism of gymnastic movements it might be well to consider briefly a few general principles which have to be reckoned with in any attempt to analyze such movements.

### GENERAL PRINCIPLES.

The principal factors—besides the force of muscular contraction—concerned in the production and modification of movement are gravity, inertia and momentum of the body or its parts, pressure in the joints (due to oblique direction of muscular pull), leverage, the resistance of fibrous substances (ligaments and fasciæ) and of passive or contracting muscles.

(1) Gravity. The weight of the body or its parts, or any weight attached to them, always acts vertically, unless we change its direction by mechanical appliances, machines, etc. It is usually antagonistic to the muscular force, though not always; e.g., in raising the arm sideways the abductors of the shoulder joint work against gravity; when lowering the arm slowly gravity is the motive force, while the abductors of the shoulder joint are still active in checking or controlling the speed of the movement. If a very quick lowering is desired, the opposite muscles, the adductors of the shoulder joint, will be called into play. Gravity of course continues to act, but this time in conjunction with the muscles. It may also be allowed to be the sole factor in the production of the movement. All that is necessary is to relax completely the abductor muscles and let the arms drop.

(2) Inertia. Besides the initial effort, differences and changes of speed must also be taken into account in estimating the power developed during a movement. An increase of speed involves more powerful muscular contraction, but of the same kind as previously; a decrease of speed, a diminution of that kind of muscular action, or perhaps a contraction of the opposite muscles, if the change of speed is sudden and marked, amounting then to a checking, and involving the overcoming of momentum.

(3) Pressure in the joints, due to oblique muscular pull. The direction of the pull of many muscles is at a very acute

angle to the (length) axis of the bone on which they pull, at least during one stage of the movement. Under such conditions a large part of the muscular force is used up in pressing the ends of the bones together, and for this reason that stage of the movement is harder than some other stage where the direction of the muscular pull is more perpendicular to the bone. Illustration: the pull of the latissimus dorsi and pectoralis major on the humerus, and of the biceps on the radius during the first part of the arm bending in the hanging position. (See also leverage.)

(4) Internal resistance. Motion in most joints is easiest within a limited range, representing only a portion (usually the central) of the total range of motion possible in the joint. Beyond this the agencies which limit motion, such as the stretching of muscles, fasciæ and ligaments, the contact of soft and bony parts, begin successively and increasingly to exert resistance. For example, bending the fingers requires an increasing amount of effort as the movement proceeds, because of the resistance offered by the extensor tendons and by the contact of the soft parts on the palmar side. Similarly, straightening of the fingers becomes increasingly difficult as we approach the straight line. In the movements of the shoulder joint and scapula, of the chest, spine and hip, the internal resistance plays an important rôle. It is one of the chief elements of difficulty in the correct execution of movements, and in the maintenance of good posture. In order to secure completeness of movement against this resistance, maximal muscular contractions of great intensity are necessary.

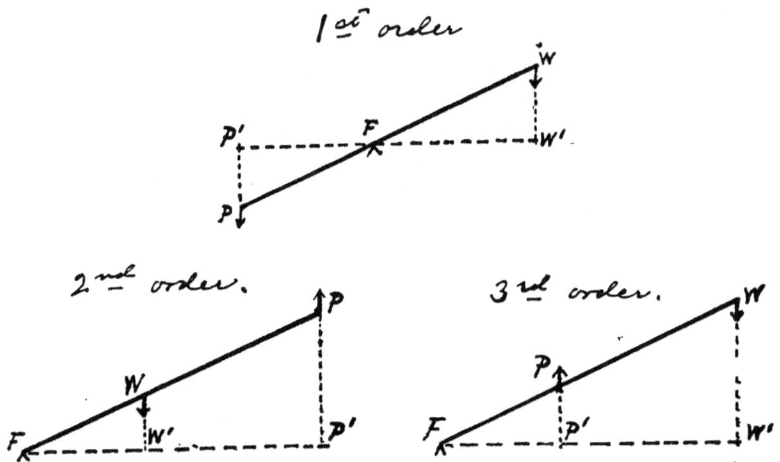


(5) Leverage. The amount of force necessary in the production of a movement or in maintaining a position depends

among other things on the relative leverage of the active muscle(s) on one hand, and of the weight on the other.  Leverage, as applied in the body, may be defined as the perpendicular distance from the axis of motion (fulcrum, joint) to the line representing the application and direction of the force.  Thus in the figure F P′ is the leverage of the power and F W′ is the leverage of the weight.  To balance, P × FP′ must equal W × FW′.

Of the three classes of levers it is probable that only the first and third are represented in the body.  Be that as it may, the usual arrangement is that resistance, i.e., the weight, reaction to gravity, etc., is applied near the distal end of a segment (bone), the power near the proximal end, close to the fulcrum (joint). The leverage of the weight is therefore much greater than the leverage of the power.  Or, stated more accurately, the power and the weight are to each other inversely as the distance from the point of application and direction of each to the axis of motion. This means that a great deal more power must be exerted by the muscles than is represented by the amount of weight they have to move or sustain.  Furthermore, the direction of application of both forces relative to the bones on which they act, and consequently their leverage, changes as the movement progresses.  This is another reason why one stage of the movement (the first in the figure) is often the hardest.  (See also obliquity of muscular pull.)

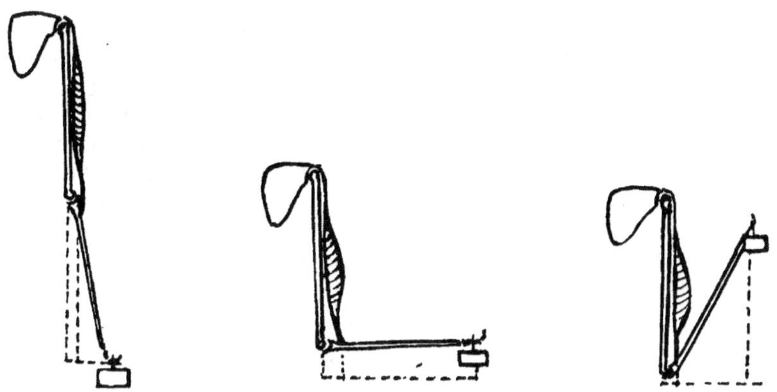

On the other hand the arc traversed by the distal end of the segment, where the weight is applied, is much greater than the arc traversed by that point on the segment where the power is applied, and as it takes the same time, the former has to travel at a much faster rate than the latter.  Thus we find that while the levers of the body are, in general, unfavorable as regards power, they are favorable for speed, and momentum; that while the muscles work at a mechanical disadvantage, as far as economy of power is concerned, rapidity of movement is greatly enhanced.

(6) Categorical classification of muscles. Finally, in analyzing the muscular action occurring in gymnastic movements, it is necessary to know not only the muscles which are directly concerned in the production of the movement—to be referred to as motor muscles—but also those which are brought into play to limit the extent and speed, and to determine the exact plane and direction of the movement. These are sometimes directly opposed to the movement, sometimes only partly so, pulling more or less obliquely in directions opposite to that in which the movement is taking place. The first may be called antagonistic, the second, steadying muscles in respect to a particular movement. Often the motor muscles themselves pull in oblique directions, then acting also as steadying muscles. Besides these kinds of muscular action there is still another; viz., the induced action of muscles attached by one end to the segment from which the motor (antagonistic and steadying) muscles take their origin, and by the other end to some distant point. This kind of action is especially marked in cases where the bone giving origin to the motor muscles is itself freely movable (as for example the scapula) and therefore requires fixation by muscular action of this secondary kind, in order to enable the motor muscles to exert the main part of their force on the distal segments (the humerus in the example given). Muscles acting in this capacity may be called fixator muscles. In many trunk and shoulder blade movements of an exact, localized character there may be several relays of such fixators, the purpose of all the complex muscular action being to produce as much and as accurate movement as possible in one place, and as little as possible anywhere else. The importance of this in the training of coördination and of the tone, strength and endurance of the muscles responsible for good posture will be readily appreciated.

## Gymnastic Movements.

### A.  FREE-STANDING ARCHING, BACK, ARM AND SHOULDER BLADE MOVEMENTS.

In defining gymnastic movements the fundamental gymnastic position will be taken as a starting point. The changes in the position of the joints will then be stated, and the action and interplay of motor, antagonistic, steadying and fixator muscles described.  The faulty tendencies peculiar to each movement will be discussed and analyzed, or at any rate the differences between the defined gymnastic movement and similar, slightly differently defined movements, gymnastic and otherwise, pointed out.

1.  *The fundamental position* of the upper part of the body is not an easy, relaxed, "natural" position.  It should be considered a gymnastic exercise and, as such, should call for a ·considerable amount of conscious muscular action (of the static kind).

The head and neck.  The line of gravitation from the head ordinarily lies in front of the thoracic spine, thus tending to make the head and neck fall forward. To prevent this the posterior neck and upper back muscles must be kept in a state of moderate contraction.  With this goes also a slight contraction of the anterior neck muscles to keep the head from being merely tilted backward, which would be the first and chief effect of the contraction of the posterior neck muscles.  By the combined and balanced action of the two sets of muscles the head is poised in a plane coincident with

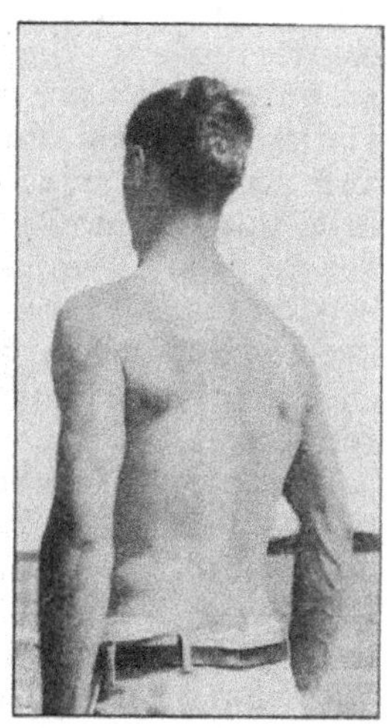

FIGURE 3.  FUNDAMENTAL GYMNASTIC POSITION

that of the "squared" shoulders.  This action will be more fully explained under "Backward bending of head."

The thoracic spine should be kept straight.  This involves a considerable amount of contraction of the longitudinal back muscles—the upper prolongations of the erector spinæ—varying in intensity according to the degree of mobility of this part of the spine in the individual, and the extent to which it is curved in the habitual, relaxed position.

The shoulders.  Placed near the top of the anteriorly concave thoracic spine they naturally tend to fall forward of their own weight until checked by the passive tension of the posterior scapular muscles (trapezii and rhomboids).  The mere straightening of the thoracic spine will in some cases put the shoulders in a fairly good, "square" position by shifting the weight line to a more posterior plane, and probably also by inducing a slight associated, unconscious action of the shoulder retractors.  But in most cases, and especially in those whose habitual position is poor for one reason or another, this is not enough, at least for a fundamental gymnastic position.  This should demand a fairly vigorous, conscious effort to depress and slightly retract the scapulæ. (The combined action of the muscles concerned in this will be discussed in connection with the shoulder and arm movements.)

The chest. As a result both of the straightening of the upper spine and the contraction of the depressors of the scapulæ which are attached to the ribs (latissimus dorsi, lower serratus magnus and pectoralis minor), the chest is held in a state of moderate expansion in the fundamental gymnastic position. This need not involve the drawing in of air, or keeping an unusual amount of air in the chest, if the abdomen is at the same time retracted.

Summary. The fundamental gymnastic position is active, consciously erect, "unnatural," in most cases. It involves fairly vigorous static contraction of all those muscles on whose tone and endurance good habitual posture depends, namely, the upper erector spinæ, the posterior and, to a less degree, the anterior neck muscles, the adductors and, more particularly, the depressors of the scapulæ as well as the abdominal muscles. The arms may be allowed to hang at the sides (not in front) comparatively relaxed, at least after the individual has learned to assume a correct position elsewhere.

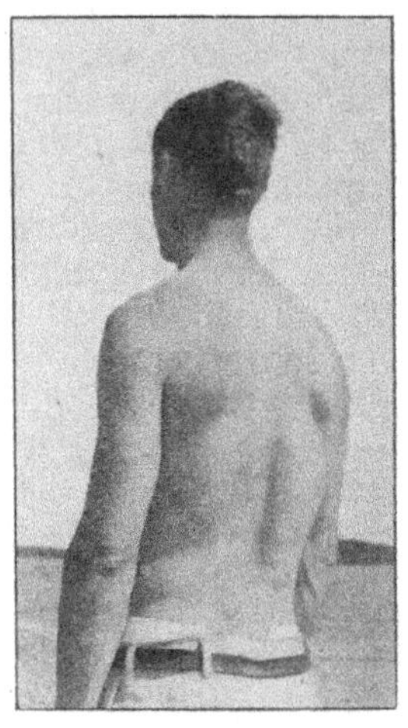

FIGURE 4. RELAXED STANDING POSITION

2. *Backward bending of head.* The muscular action is of the same kind as that given for the fundamental standing position, but it is of greater intensity, especially in the case of the longitudinal back and posterior neck muscles. The majority of the latter are attached to the upper part of the cervical spine, and many to the occiput. Because of this, and also because the cervical spine is naturally hyperextended, i.e., convex anteriorly, the effect of strong contraction of the posterior neck muscles is to tilt the head backward, that is, to increase the hyperextension in the cervical spine and at the same time to hyperextend the head on the atlas. Such a movement is of very small value, as the head may still be, and very often is, in front of the plane of the

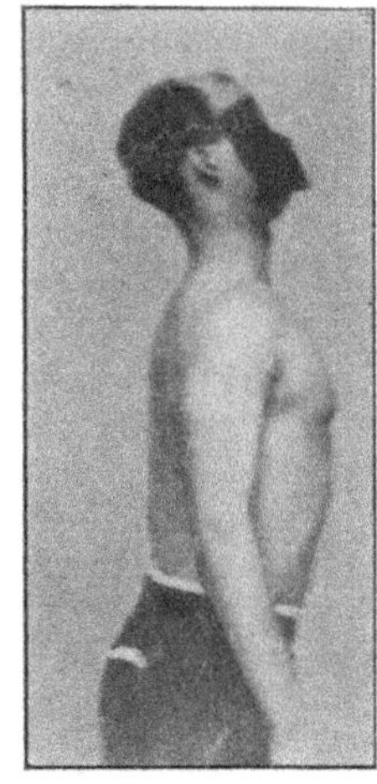

FIGURE 5. BACKWARD BENDING OF HEAD

shoulders. To avoid this, and to obtain a good poise of the head, the flexors of the head and neck (rectus capitis anticus major and minor, longus colli, scaleni and the small muscles running between the sternum, hyoid bone and lower jaw) must be strongly contracted. This is what occurs when the effort is made to "draw in the chin." The two sets of muscles thus working against each other, the posterior slightly in excess of the anterior, keep the head steady on the top of the cervical spine, produce a straightening of the latter, bind the two firmly together and make them move backward as one piece. In other words, the pull of the posterior muscles, upper back as well as neck, is in this way made to produce a backward movement of the whole neck, with the head, and is in reality an extension in the upper thoracic spine. It is valuable not only for the cultivation of a good posture of the head and for improving the musculature of the neck, but by inducing straightening of the upper thoracic spine it also leads to moderate expansion of the upper chest. This is made more pronounced by (1) the pull of the sterno-mastoids and the other anterior neck muscles attached by their lower ends to the sternum and two upper ribs; (2) by the contraction of the shoulder blade depressors. These are brought into play in order to keep the shoulders from moving upward, a tendency which is very strong because some of the posterior neck muscles (trapezius and lev. ang. scap.) are also elevators of the shoulder blades. When they contract vigorously in the effort to move the head backward, they also tend to pull the scapula up towards the head, unless this action is neutralized and the

scapula held fixed by the depressors of the latter, viz., the latissimus dorsi, lower serratus magnus, pectoralis minor. These again are attached by their lower ends to the sides and front of the chest, from the third to the twelfth ribs, and as their pull is more or less upward, they will contribute materially to, and make more general, the chest expansion which results in the first place from the straightening of the (upper) thoracic spine.

3. *Backward bending of trunk.* The mechanism of this is practically the same as that of the preceding. The muscular contractions should be of the utmost intensity, however, thereby insuring the most complete extension in

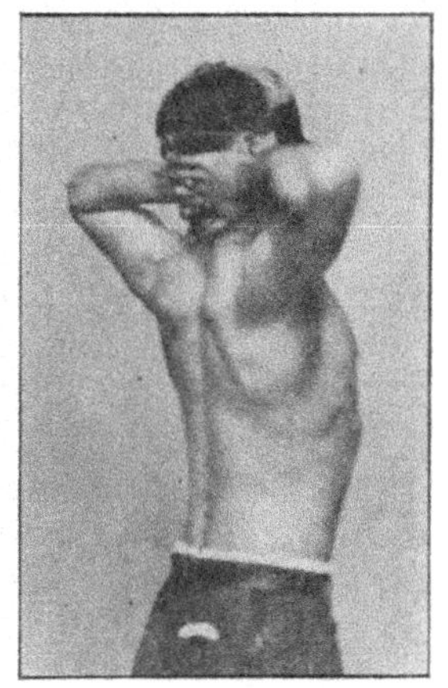

the thoracic spine of which this region is capable. Efforts should be made to localize the movement high up and to minimize the participation of the lumbar spine. Very few persons are able to do this by *limiting the muscular contraction* to the upper portion of the erector spinæ, this group usually contracting as a whole. Its lower portion is more compact and powerful than the upper; it runs over that part of the spine which enjoys the greatest freedom of motion, especially in a backward direction, and which is already in a state of hyperextension (concave backward) and therefore offers the muscle better leverage than the posteriorly convex thoracic region. Gravity, too, soon becomes a factor and acts with increasing leverage as the arching in the lower back becomes more pronounced. In short, any strong effort to arch backward, even when directions regarding localization high up are most explicit, is apt to result in a marked hyperextension of the lumbar region, often without even including the full amount of straightening possible in the thoracic spine, which is the main object of the exercise. The more untrained the individual, the more this is the case. In extreme instances of this inability to localize, even the knee joints participate in· the movement. It is for this reason that it is always unsatisfactory and inadvisable to attempt a "backward bending of the trunk" with classes or individuals until they have learned, by practicing backward bending of head, to make the muscular effort high up in the back, and also to neutralize the action of the lower erector spinæ, gravity, etc., by strongly retracting the abdomen and by holding the pelvis in a more horizontal plane than in the ordinary position. In this way the lumbar hyperextension may be reduced to a minimum, indeed entirely prevented in many cases. This, however, is difficult to teach a person, and requires persistent and patient instruction and assistance. This subject will come up again in the chapter on the lower trunk and hip region.

With the extreme contraction of the back extensors should be associated, by way of reinforcement, equally powerful action of the posterior scapular muscles, i.e., the adductors and especially the depressors of the shoulder blades. As has already been

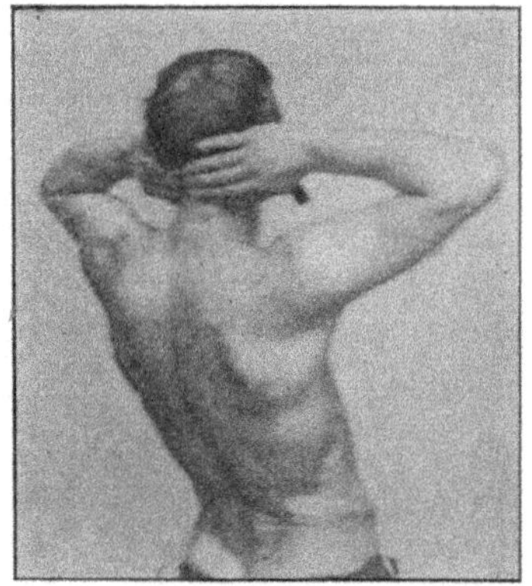

FIGURE 7. FAULTY BACKWARD BENDING OF TRUNK

stated, the latter are at the same time elevators of the ribs, and as the scapulæ cannot move very far downward; the effect of the pull of these muscles will be to raise the ten lower ribs. The subclavius (an indirect depressor of scapula) and the anterior neck muscles, which are both being stretched and trying to contract, do the same for the two upper ribs. The complete straightening of the thoracic spine is always accompanied by a considerable expansion of the chest through the stretching of costovertebral ligaments. All these factors taken together bring about an extreme excursion of the ribs upward and only to a slightly less extent laterally.

4. *Forward bending of trunk.* This movement should take place chiefly in the hip joints, but should also include some flexion in the lumbar region, enough to obliterate the natural hyperextension there and make the whole spine approach as nearly as possible a straight line with an inclination of about forty-five de-

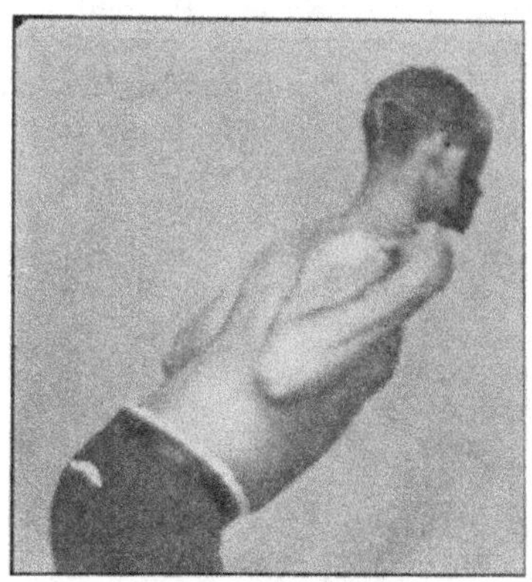

FIGURE 8. FORWARD BENDING OF TRUNK. ALSO ARM BENDING

grees. The most important muscular action occurs, however, in the upper back.

The movement is started by a slight contraction of the abdominal muscles and continued by gravity. All the back muscles as well as the posterior hip muscles are then brought into action; the latter to control the speed of the movement in the hip joints, the former to keep the spine straight and rigid. As the inclination increases, the leverage of the weight becomes greater, and the muscles mentioned work at a correspondingly increasing mechanical disadvantage. Hence the strong tendency to allow the upper back to curve and the head and shoulders to droop. This tendency is the stronger the higher the arms are held, both because the center of gravity is thereby raised, with a corresponding increase of the weight leverage, and also because of the additional work demanded of the posterior shoulder blade muscles.

Another factor which adds to the difficulty of keeping the upper back straight in this movement is the inability, especially in untrained individuals, to keep the upper back muscles in a state of strong, unyielding static contraction, while the lower erector spinæ and the posterior hip muscles are allowed to yield gradually. This is sometimes called "eccentric" contraction. All these muscles, and especially the longitudinal back muscles, are closely associated and usually work together as a physiological whole. It is doubtful if a segment of these at lower level can remain relaxed while one at a higher level is contracting vigorously. But by practice a person may learn to contract different portions with different degrees of intensity. This seems to be what happens in forward bending of trunk when done correctly as described. The same is probably true to some extent in the preceding movements, backward bending of head and trunk, and in the fundamental gymnastic position.

In returning to the erect position the same muscles are active, the lower erector spinæ and the hip extensors now becoming the motor force, contracting "concentrically" (shortening), while gravity, acting with a diminishing leverage as the movement proceeds, is the antagonistic force.

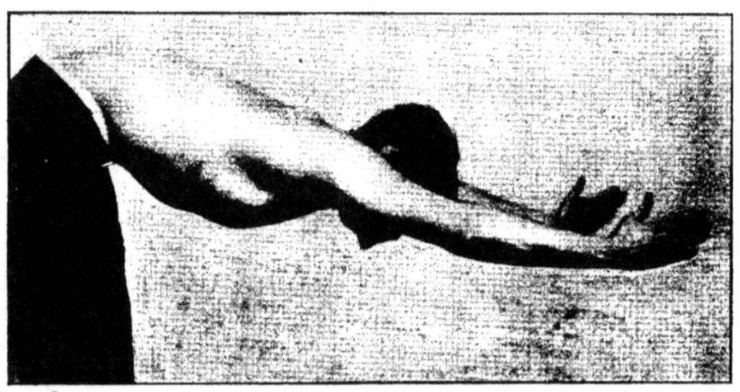

FIGURE 9. FORWARD-DOWNWARD BENDING OF TRUNK

5. *Forward-downward bending of trunk* is like the preceding in all respects, except that the lumbar and hip joint flexion is carried as far as possible, by relaxing the lower back muscles and hip joint extensors. This should be done without disturbing the position of the upper back by induced relaxation of the upper back and posterior shoulder blade muscles.

Here, as in the preceding movement, the chest is kept in the fundamental position. This is here even more difficult than in forward bending, because of the stronger tendency to curve the upper back. The movement should not be allowed to proceed far enough, nor should the arms be held in a position high enough to induce this curving of the upper back with the associated depression of the chest.

The two movements are of value in/training the control, strength, tone and endurance of all the back muscles; by making them do their full duty in maintaining erect posture under difficulties, which may be as great as one wishes. Moreover, the conditions in the lower back as regards pressure and tension are reversed, thus serving, in a measure, to counteract the undesirable effects of excessive lumbar hyperextension often obtaining in the habitual standing position and in many gymnastic exercises.

6. *Arm bending.* This movement is done in various ways: with elbows on a level with the shoulder; with hands placed on the chest; with hands in front of the shoulders and elbows either close to the waist, or behind the lateral plane of the body, or directly in front (the last is often seen when chest weights are used); with elbows approximately at right angles, close to the waist, and forearms directed horizontally forward; finally with elbows completely flexed, as close to the body as possible, and hands (clenched or not) as far back on the shoulders as possible. The last variation will be analyzed, embodying as it does all the valuable features of the others and being the most vigorous and effective of them all. (Fig. 8.)

The joint mechanism is comparatively simple: complete flexion in the elbow joint, and complete rotation outward in the shoulder joint. The motor muscles are the forearm flexors (biceps, supinator longus, brachialis anticus) and the rotators outward of the upper arm (infraspinatus, teres minor and the posterior portion of the deltoid). It is the complete rotation outward in the shoulder joint that makes the movement effective and its analysis interesting.

It is difficult for most persons to place the hands close to and on the outside of the shoulder and at the same time keep the elbows close to the waist. In other words, with the effort at complete flexion in the elbow and complete rotation outward in the shoulder joint there is associated an almost irresistible tendency to abduction in the shoulder joint and rotation upward of the scapula. The former is probably caused by the action of the biceps (as one of the forearm flexors), one of whose heads also abducts the shoulder joint, and by the induced action of the whole deltoid, whose posterior portion helps in producing the rotation outward in the shoulder joint. The rotation upward of scapula, which always to some extent accompanies abduction in the shoulder joint, is due principally to the pull of teres major. This, being a rotator inward of the shoulder joint, is of course stretched during rotation outward. It also contracts in the effort to keep the elbow close to the side of the body. Being attached by its lower end to or near the lower angle of the scapula, its effort to adduct the arm results partly in swinging the lower angle of the scapula outward, toward the humerus. In this position of the shoulder joint the teres minor has a similar though weaker action, when it contracts as a rotator outward.

In the effort to keep the shoulder joint adducted, the latissimus dorsi is also brought into play. This pulls the arm backward, as well as downward and inward, and is thus largely responsible for another of the common "faults" of the movement, viz., the passing of the elbow behind the plane of the back. At the same. time this muscle, like the teres major, is a rotator inward and contributes a large part of the resistance the outward rotators have to overcome. When to this is added the resistance offered by the other rotators inward, teres major, subscapularis and pectoralis major, the difficulty of complete rotation outward is explained.

To insure a complete and "pure" movement as defined at the outset, it is then necessary to employ still other muscles. In the first place, the motor muscles—teres minor, infraspinatus and posterior deltoid—have to contract with utmost vigor to overcome the resistance of the antagonistic and steadying muscles as decribed above. On account of the extreme effort which this demands, the trapezius and perhaps to a less extent the rhomboids contract "in sympathy," tending to move the scapula nearer the spine, in this way reinforcing the rotators outward of the shoulder joint. In this action the adductors of the scapula and the rotators outward of the shoulder joint may be considered as one physiological whole, with the scapula placed at its lower and outer portion, and attached at its outer end to the greater tuberosity of the humerus. Secondly, the strong effort needed to keep the elbow down close to the side, i.e., to keep the arm adducted, leads to the associated contraction of all the shoulder blade depressors— the pectoralis minor, lower pectoralis major and lower serratus magnus, as well as the latissimus dorsi (acting in the first place as an adductor of the arm) and the lower trapezius (already mentioned as taking part in the effort at adduction of the scapula). The action of the pectoralis major neutralizes the tendency of the latissimus dorsi and teres major to pull the arm too far backward.

Besides bringing about the "pure" and complete movement of arm bending according to the definition given, the result of the contraction of all these muscles in the way described is a very forcible expansion of the chest, both antero-posteriorly and laterally. Some of the reasons for this are the same as those already described under "Backward bending of trunk," viz., the pull of the shoulder blade depressors on the ten lower ribs. In addition, the lower pectoralis major, while helping to hold the arm down and keeping it from moving behind the lateral plane of the body, is at the same time stretched by the rotation outward in the shoulder joint. Being kept by other muscles from moving the arm forward and rotating inward it tends to move the points of its lower attachment (the cartilages of the fifth, sixth and seventh ribs) upward and outward. The direction of the fibers of this portion of the muscle is oblique enough to enable it to act in this way, and so help to intensify the enlargement of this part of the chest.

Another effect of doing the movement in the way described is a marked extension of the thoracic and lumbar regions of the spine. Some of this is caused by the forcible elevation and eversion of the ribs, but aside from this the strong efforts of the posterior shoulder muscles induce an almost involuntary contraction of the extensors of the spine. This may, indeed, be the primary factor, especially if the attention and efforts of the individual are directed to it. Such admonitions are often necessary to insure a good posture of the head. In any case, the contraction of the longitudinal back muscles, as has already been shown, cannot be localized very definitely to the higher levels, and almost invariably produces the most marked effects in the lower back. This excessive hyperextension, which may reach as high up as the tenth thoracic vertebra, and even higher in exceptional cases, is no doubt also contributed to by the latissimus dorsi, as the majority of its fibres arise from the lower thoracic and the whole lumbar spine, and pass obliquely upward, outward and forward. Not being permitted to pull its upper attachment (on the humerus) backward because of the resistance of the pectoralis major, it tends to pull its lower attachment (lumbar spine) forward.

This excessive "hollowing" of the lower back is a very undesirable by-product of the movement. It is considered serious enough by many teachers to justify them in so defining it as to leave out the complete rotation outward or the complete adduction in the shoulder joint, or both. It then assumes the form of one or another of the variations enumerated in the beginning, some of which were designated as "faulty" later in the discussion. This point of view is of course entirely reasonable. But on the other hand it is probably safe to say that with these two elements left out the movement loses most of its effectiveness, both as regards the amount and vigor of the muscular work done, and the kind of training—in tone, endurance and control—given to those muscles which are responsible for good posture of the upper back, chest and shoulders. Furthermore, it is possible to do the movement with utmost vigor and completeness without inducing much, or any, hyperextension in the lower back. While this is difficult and requires the additional action of the abdominal muscles and hip extensors, the necessary amount of coördination is attainable by the average individual, if he is properly guided and stimulated by the teacher. When this neutralizing muscular action is mastered, the all-round value, as well as the complexity, of this useful and apparently simple movement is still further increased. This part of the mechanism of the movement has already been alluded to under "Backward bending of trunk," and will be further explained in the chapter on the lower trunk and hip regions.

7. *Arm raising sideways.* The arms are moved through or rather behind the lateral plane of the body to the horizontal position, palms down. Anatomically that means abduction in the shoulder joint with some rotation upward of the scapula and efforts to adduct and depress this bone.

The rotation upward of the scapula in this movement illustrates something which has already been alluded to, namely, the tendency of the scapula to follow the arm. Normally the shoulder joint allows at least 100 degrees of abduction. Theoretically, therefore, there should be no need of the scapula taking part in this movement (arm raising sideways). The earlier investigators of the mechanism of movements (the brothers Weber) assumed that any extensive movement of the arm involved first the shoulder joint only, and then, when the limits of motion in that joint had been reached (ligaments being stretched, etc.), the scapula, with the arm firmly fixed to it, became the moving segment. That this is not the case can be readily demonstrated by any one, and has been definitely proved by Steinhausen. He has shown, by a series of radiographs, that the scapular element is actually most pronounced in the early stages of a movement of the arm away from the side and up overhead. In general it may be said that all arm movements involve displacements of the scapula, and even when efforts are made to avoid it, this bone will begin to move long before the extreme limits of motion in the shoulder joint have been reached. This can be due only to two factors: (1) the intimate muscular connections between the humerus and scapula, the muscles acting as elastic ligaments of the shoulder joint; and (2) induced or associated contraction of scapular muscles whenever any set of shoulder joint muscles contracts vigorously. Illustration of both was afforded in the analysis of the preceding movement "Arm bending." In "Arm raising sideways" we have an even simpler case.

The abduction in the shoulder joint is produced by the deltoid and supraspinatus, aided by the long head of the biceps. As soon as the arm begins to move, the muscles running from the lower angle of the scapula to the humerus—teres major, teres minor and the lower fibers of the subscapularis, especially the teres major—are made tense and so exert an outward pull on the lower angle of the scapula. On the other hand, the deltoid is so closely associated with the trapezius, functionally, that it is practically impossible to contract the former without inducing contraction of at least the upper portion of the latter. Here again it will be helpful to consider the two muscles one, physiologically, with the clavicle and upper part of the scapula set into its middle. In any upward movement of the arm the two work together. All parts of the trapezius pull the upper end of the scapula toward the spine more than the lower end. This, then, with the swinging outward of the lower angle by the passive pull of the teres major, etc., accounts for the rotation upward of the scapula. The lower and middle parts of the serratus magnus also contract, being habitually associated with the trapezius in rotation upward of the scapula (Mollier).

The upper trapezius, on account of its oblique direction, is also a scapular elevator. This accounts, in part, for the common tendency to raise the shoulders, as well as the arms, in this movement, especially when no particular effort is made to prevent it.

The plane of the movement is determined chiefly by the relative amount of resistance offered by the antagonistic muscles—pectoralis major on the one hand, and latissimus dorsi and teres major on the other. Without explicit directions the average individual will move the arms in front of, rather than through or behind, the lateral plane of the body. This is the easiest way, and does not require any special effort. The pectoral pulls in a more horizontal direction forward than the latissimus dorsi and teres major do in a backward direction. In other words, the pectoral has the advantage in leverage and directness of pull over the others. Besides it is apt to have greater tone—less slack to be taken up, so to speak.

So far, then, the mechanism of the movement represents only what occurs in an ordinary, non-gymnastic arm raising sideways, such as we do many times in the course of the day without thinking about it. Such a movement would require but little muscular work and still less muscular control. To make it amount to anything in these respects, that is, to make it a gymnastic exercise, it must be done according to the definition given at the outset: arms moving behind the transverse plane of the body. This implies additional muscular work, and work of an exact character. The tendency to let the arm move forward is overcome by active contraction of the latissimus dorsi and teres major. Associated with this and inseparable from it, is the effort to adduct the scapula by vigorous contraction of the whole trapezius and the rhomboids. There is also induced action of the levator anguli scapulæ. With the extreme contraction of the posterior deltoid, the arm is thus brought back as far as possible. But the upper trapezius, rhomboids (and levator anguli scapulæ) are elevators as well as adductors of the scapula, because of the oblique direction of their fibers. Hence the raising of the shoulders, already mentioned as occurring even in the easy "non-gymnastic" form of the movement, when the upper trapezius contracts "in sympathy" with the deltoid, tends to become more pronounced. Especially is this the case if the movement is done quickly. For this reason special effort has to be made to keep the shoulders down. This involves additional action of the latissimus dorsi and the lower trapezius (both already active in the effort to keep the arms back) as well as the pectoralis minor, lower pectoralis major and lower serratus magnus (see next movement for more detailed analysis of the interplay of elevators and depressors).

The pectoralis minor and (lower) serratus magnus are abductors as well as depressors of the scapula. When they are made to work against the adductors for the purpose of keeping the shoulders down, there results also a "flattening" of the upper back, i.e., a closer apposition of the vertebral borders of the scapulæ to the back. The latissimus dorsi, lower serratus magnus and pectoralis minor are attached by their lower ends to the ten lower ribs. When the scapula and arm have been fixed, or moved as far as is desired, further action of these muscles will produce chest expansion.

The total result, then, of the contraction of all these muscles in the way described is to move the arms to the horizontal position in a plane well behind the shoulders without raising the latter, and besides, to bring about a "flattening" of the upper back and a moderate chest expansion. This is accompanied, as usual, by a straightening of the upper back. To make the latter as pronounced as possible, the head must be maintained in the fundamental, erect posture, and without special effort this is apt to be lost to some extent.

In returning to the fundamental position the same muscles are still active, but the abductors of the shoulder joint and the rotators upward of the scapula are allowed to yield to gravity, which is the motor force if the movement is slow, or to the adductors of the shoulder joint and the rotators downward of the scapula if the movement is quick.

8. *Forward bending of arms* differs from the preceding only in the additional complete flexion of the elbows. This brings the hands in front of and on a level with the shoulders. Here again, conscious effort has to be made to keep the elbows well back and

the shoulders down. In other words, the action of the motor muscles—deltoid, supraspinatus (and biceps)—must be supplemented by vigorous contraction of the adductors and depressors of the scapula in order to execute the movement properly.

The repeated mention of these two sets of muscles in the gymnastic exercises so far analyzed has undoubtedly been noted by the reader. Their forcible action and orderly, controlled interplay with each other and with their antagonists, the elevators and abductors of the scapula, are, or should be, a constant and marked feature of all gymnastic

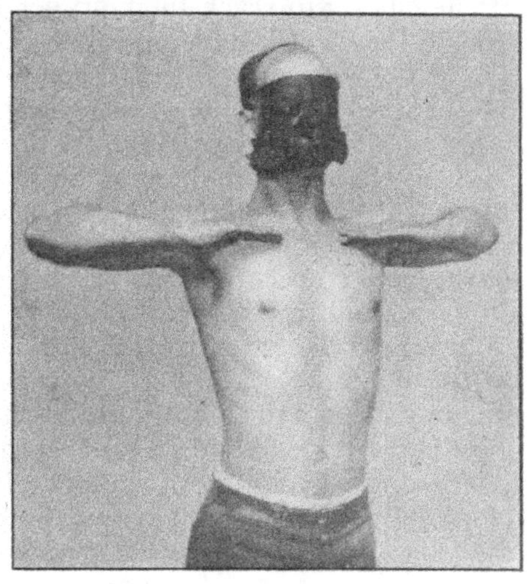

FIGURE 10.  FORWARD BENDING OF ARMS

exercises and especially in movements of the upper part of the body. In the exercises already described, and in those that are to follow, the definitions are such as always to make this element prominent by presenting varying degrees of difficulty and resistance to the properly coördinated action of these muscles. As has already several times been stated, by so doing, well-controlled and powerful action of the longitudinal back muscles is also induced. The ultimate object of defining movements in this way will be discussed in the final chapter (on fixation, localization, muscular tone, etc.).

The movement "Forward bending of arms" may, perhaps, better than any other serve to illustrate still further the combined and at the same time partially antagonistic action of the shoulder blade muscles. While it offers a fair degree of difficulty to correct execution, it is less marked in this respect than some of the movements to be described, because of the absence of rotation in the shoulder joint. For the same reason its analysis is less complicated.

The strong contraction of the scapular adductors—trapezius, levator anguli scapulæ,* rhomboids (direct) and latissimus dorsi

---

*The lev. ang. scap. has probably little, if any, adductory action on the scapula. It is chiefly an elevator and also helps in rotation downward of the scapula. As such it is always associated with the rhomboids and upper trapezius.

(indirect)—associated with the effort to keep the elbows back, is very apt to result also in a raising of the shoulders and a failure of the elbows to reach their proper level. The reason for this is that all the direct adductors, with the exception of the lower portion of the trapezius, are also elevators of the scapula. On the whole, they are perhaps more favorably situated for the production of elevation than of adduction. Of the direct adductors the lower trapezius alone opposes this tendency to elevation. To reënforce it the latissimus dorsi, an indirect depressor, as well as adductor, of the scapula (through its pull on the humerus) is brought into action.

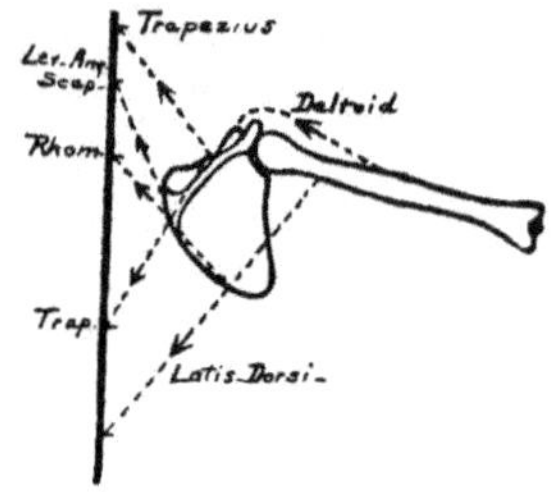


But as its leverage on the humerus in this position of the shoulder joint is fairly good and its pull on this bone almost perpendicular, a large part of its work is spent in opposition to the shoulder joint abductors—deltoid, supraspinatus and biceps. These are working at a mechanical disadvantage on account of their oblique pull on the humerus, and they are, besides, very nearly at the end of their contracting range (the biceps is probably not of much use here as a shoulder joint abductor, because its whole range of contraction is needed for the flexion of the elbow). As a consequence the latissimus dorsi is apt to get the better of the shoulder joint abductors and prevent them from raising the arm to the horizontal position. In other words, the latissimus fails to help the lower trapezius in its effort to depress the scapula, and does something which is literally, as well as figuratively, "more in its line"; it adducts the humerus, which is its direct function. It also pulls the arm backward as far as it will go (by a movement in the nature of hyperextension) in the shoulder joint, and after that of course adducts the scapula.

To get the elbow up to the proper level and at the same time keep the shoulder from raising as a result of the excessive upward pull of the upper scapular adductors, one of two things must take place. Either the supraspinatus and deltoid must contract with sufficient intensity to overcome the excessive pull of the latissimus, so that the elbow may be brought up to the level of and behind the shoulder and kept there, and the pull of the latissimus thereby be exerted on the scapula; or additional scapular depressors must be called upon. Probably both of these means are used by the average individual, at least in the beginning of gymnastic training, and this is in fact what is desired.

The other scapular depressors are the pectoralis minor and lower serratus magnus (direct) and the lower pectoralis major (indirect).* The lower pectoralis major, like the latissimus, and for the same reason, partly resists the deltoid and supraspinatus and so tends to pull the arm, instead of the scapula, down; but unlike the latissimus and in opposition to it, it also pulls the arm forward, and, through its pull on the arm, tends to abduct the scapula as well. Its success as a depressor of the scapula is, then, as in the case of the latissimus, dependent on the ability of the deltoid and supraspinatus to raise the arm to, and hold it in, a horizontal position. The pectoralis minor and lower serratus magnus must, therefore, finally be called into action to insure the fixation of the scapula as far as elevation is concerned. These, being also abductors, will by their contraction materially add to the resistance already exerted by the pectoralis major against the scapular adductors. The latter, it will be remembered, are brought into action in the first place in order to reënforce the posterior deltoid in its effort to get the arm back.

To sum up, then, the complete and "pure" movement of Forward bending of arms" is accomplished only by the extreme contraction of the shoulder joint abductors—deltoid, supraspinatus and biceps. The plane of the movement behind the back is further insured by the active resistance of the latissimus dorsi, while the scapula is fixed by the contraction of its depressors and adductors against its elevators and abductors, the former set slightly in excess of the latter. There will be some rotation upward of the scapula, as the trapezius and serratus magnus are both active, and the teres major is at any rate in a state of tension, but this rotation upward will not be as great as would be the case if all the scapular muscles (including the rotators downward) were not vigorously contracted.

The incidental, but really most important, result of the muscular action here, as in the exercises previously described, is a flattening and straightening of the upper back, with accompanying chest expansion. This, it will be remembered, is due to the attachment of the scapular depressors to the ribs, and is made more pronounced by the induced contraction of the erector spinæ group.

The proper muscular coordination in this movement seems to be more difficult, at least to a beginner, than in the preceding movement, "Arm raising sideways. The "faults"—elevation of the shoulders and drooping of the arms—are more common and persistent in the former than in the latter. The addition of such an apparently insignificant element as flexion of the elbows hardly seems enough to account for the difference, especially as at first

---

*The subclavius is also a depressor, but being so small and insignificant it will not be enumerated hereafter. It will be understood to be included whenever the scapular depressors are mentioned.

sight it might appear to make the movement easier by reducing the weight leverage. Still, the increase in complexity is real. To keep the wrists straight, and the hands, elbows and shoulders on the same level, and this as low as possible, probably requires more divided attention, and undoubtedly more coördination, than keeping all the segments of the limb in line and on the same lever. The small amount of help given by the biceps in the abduction of the shoulder joint, because of its complete contraction to produce flexion in the elbow, may also be a factor.

With a little practice the average individual soon learns to do "Forward bending of arms," correctly, in the main, with comparative ease. This saving in effort is probably due to acquired ability to contract the deltoid, especially its posterior portion, and the lower trapezius more powerfully, while the contraction of the upper trapezius, rhomboids and levator anguli scapulæ is to some extent inhibited. This makes vigorous action of the latissimus, serratus magnus and pectoralis less necessary. The contraction of the last named may indeed be almost entirely dispensed with in the case of a well-trained individual. In gymnastic practice, however, it is well always to demand sufficient vigor in doing the exercise to call forth a fair degree of action of the depressors and adductors of the scapula and the extensors of the spine. This may be accomplished in various ways, such as by direct stimulation of the class, or by combining the movement with a trunk or leg movement.

9. *Arm raising sideways with palms up.* The first part of this movement has already been described (see "Arm raising sideways"). The additional element involves complete rotation outward in the shoulder joint and complete supination of the forearm. The action of motor, steadying and fixator muscles in complete rotation outward in the shoulder joint is similar to that occurring in "Arm bending" (see page 28). The rotation upward of the scapula, which is to some extent associated with each part of the movement when done separately, is more pronounced when they are combined. The same is true in a less degree of the elevation of the scapula. Hence the efforts to resist these scapular displacements must be correspondingly vigorous. The net result is a more perfect flattening of the back and a greater lateral chest expansion than in any of the preceding movements.

10. *Half sideways bending of arms.* This differs from the preceding only in that the elbows are bent to right angle. The increase in difficulty of execution is, however, out of all proportion to the relatively slight change in joint mechanism. Here the tendency to raise the shoulders and to lower the elbows is even greater than in "Forward bending of arms." The reasons

for this are probably (1) the lessened availability of the biceps for use as an abductor of the arm, most of its "contracting range"

being needed **for** flexion of the elbow and supination of the forearm; (2) the absence of "landmarks" as guides to the museular sense, the position reached by the movement being of an intermediate character with possibility of displacement in every direction except backward. In "Arm bending" (see page 28) the efforts to adduct the arm and depress the scapula are associated and are continued until each meets .absolute

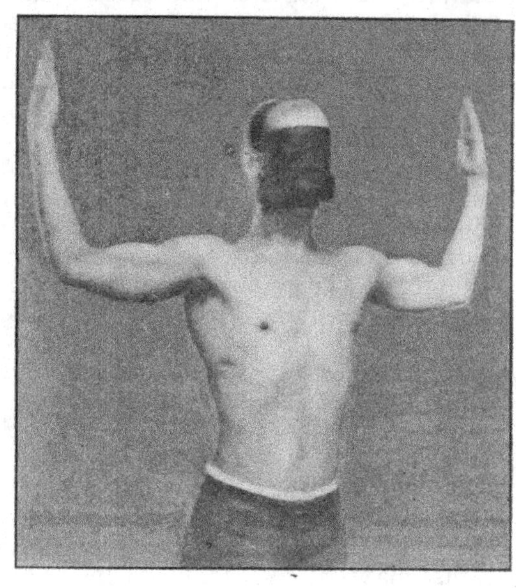

Fig. 11.   Half Sideways Bending of Arms

resistance.   Here efforts to depress the scapula must be made while the somewhat contrary movement of abduction, as well as rotation outward, of the arm is taking place.   The difficulties which this gives rise to were discussed at length under "Forward bending of arms."   Here, too, the additional attention and coördination, as well as the actual muscular work required to find and hold the right angle at the elbow and to keep the forearm in full supination, still further increase the difficulties.   For these reasons the movement is not suitable for beginners.   But when the proper coördination has been acquired, it is an excellent test of the individual's control of all the upper trunk and shoulder muscles, as well as an effective agent for further cultivation of the control, endurance and tone of those muscles.

11.   *Placing the hands behind the neck* (without locking the fingers) with elbows as far back as possible, and the head maintained in the fundamental position.   (Fig. 6.)   While somewhat similar to the preceding, it is not nearly as difficult.   The joint mechanism is like that of "Forward bending of arms," viz., abduction in the shoulder joint, rotation upward of the scapula and flexion in the elbow, plus complete rotation outward in the shoulder joint.   The muscular action, while greater in amount

and apparently more complex than in "Forward bending of arms" because of the additional action of the outward shoulder joint rotators—infraspinatus and teres minor—is really less difficult. This is due, partly at least, to the greater ease of "finding" and even maintaining the terminal position, the contact of the hands with the neck serving as a readily available and familiar guide to the proper muscular efforts. On this account it is easier to keep the shoulders down without lowering the elbows, and the individual can concentrate his attention and efforts on keeping the elbows well back. This, while involving hard work, is here a simpler problem in coördination than the corresponding effort in "Forward bending of arms." The shoulder joint abductors—deltoid and supraspinatus—and the scapular adductors—trapezius, rhomboids and latissimus dorsi—are here able to work in more perfect unison, because, by the outward rotation of the arm, the pull of the former, and especially of the posterior and central portions of the deltoid, is changed from the direct lateral plane to an oblique upward and backward direction. This is more nearly in line with the pull of the scapular adductors.

In this movement, as in "Arm bending," in "Half sideways bending of arms" and in "Arm raising sideways with palms up," the complete rotation outward in the shoulder joint requires intense maximal contraction of the relatively small outward rotators—infraspinatus and teres minor. The resistance offered by the more numerous and stronger inward rotators—latissimus dorsi, teres major, subscapularis and pectoralis major—is considerable even in the fundamental position of the joint. It increases rapidly as the arm is raised and at the same time moved backward. The anterior part of the capsular ligament with its accessory band, the coraco-humeral ligament, is also made tense during the last stage of the rotation outward. In individuals whose ligaments are short and whose inward rotators are of relatively excessive tone—and such cases are numerous—the amount of rotation outward is often much reduced. When, for any reason, rotation outward in this movement is incomplete, the hands cannot be brought behind the neck—unless the head (and neck), or the elbows, are moved forward. By moving the head forward to meet the hands and then backward again to the fundamental position, the posterior neck muscles are made to reënforce the rotators outward of the shoulder joint. To make this possible the wrist and hand must be kept straight and rigid, and the elbow must not be allowed to move forward. In this way the forearm becomes the lever through which the force of the contraction of the neck muscles is transmitted to the arm. If the head is kept erect from the outset, and the elbows are first moved forward, then backward, the same result is obtained.

When the amount of rotation outward in the shoulder joint is less than normal, or the outward rotators contract insufficiently, one of three things happens: the head is not brought back to the fundamental position; or, if it is, the elbows are allowed to remain forward, thereby relaxing somewhat the muscles (especially the pectoralis major) and ligaments which resist rotation outward; finally, if the individual exerts himself with sufficient vigor to keep both the head and elbows back, the wrists and hands yield, assume a position of hyperextension and instead of meeting in a straight line, behind the neck, converge to this point by a more or less acute angle. If a compromise must be made, the last-mentioned expedient is the least objectionable. Persistent and conscientious efforts will in most cases lead to a sufficient stretching of the antagonistic structures and strengthening of the outward rotators of the shoulder joint to enable the individual to assume and maintain the correct terminal position of this movement. While this process of adjustment is going on it is best to make sure of the position of the head and elbows (shoulders) first, and gradually get the wrists and hands straighter. In this way the scapular adductors and depressors, and the upper erector spinæ are given opportunity for complete and powerful contraction each time the position is taken, and this, as we have seen, means straightening and flattening of the back, as well as forcible chest expansion.

The movement and the position reached at the end of it are very useful as parts of compound movements in which the other elements may be trunk or leg movements. In trunk movements, such as forward and backward bendings, side bendings and twistings, the position adds to the severity and difficulty of the muscular work on the one hand, but on the other it helps the individual to judge the direction and plane of the trunk movement, and so in a way facilitates correct execution. The terminal position, when correctly taken, also has a certain element of stability—everything having been moved as far as possible—and this, too, favors accurate localization and completeness of movement elsewhere.

12. *Arm raising sideways—upward.* The first part of this movement has already been discussed under "Arm raising sideways" with palms down, the second part—the turning of the hands—under "Arm raising sideways with palms up." The mechanism of the latter (which includes that of the former) involves incomplete abduction and complete rotation outward in the shoulder joint, and partial rotation upward of the scapula, accomplished by the action of the corresponding muscles, namely, the deltoid and supraspinatus, infraspinatus and teres minor,

trapezius and serratus magnus. Besides, the action of the adductors and depressors of the scapula was shown to be an essential feature of these exercises, in order to minimize the displacement of the shoulder blade and confine the movement as much as possible to the shoulder joint.

From this point on the movement consists of a completion of the abduction in the shoulder joint and of the rotation upward of the scapula. The motor muscles are therefore the same as before. They simply contract more completely and powerfully. The same is true of the antagonistic and steadying muscles. Of the latter, the latissimus dorsi and the rhomboids must contract with considerable force, as they share with the central and posterior deltoid and the trapezius (motor muscles) the responsibility in guiding the movement in (or better behind) the lateral plane of the body by keeping the scapula well adducted.

The terminal position (Fig. 12.) involves then the full range of motion in all the joints of the shoulder girdle, and is a very fair index of the mobility in those joints. When this is limited for any reason, such as short, tight ligaments, or excessive tone or contracture of some of the muscles (usually the anterior), the arms cannot be brought to a vertical position. The resistance being strongest in front, on account of the tension of the adductors and rotators inward of the shoulder joint—(latissimus) teres major, pectoralis major and subscapularis, as well as the pectoralis minor, which resists the rotation upward of the scapula—there is a marked tendency of the arms to move forward as they ascend. There is also a strong inclination to turn the palms forward, instead of toward each other. This means incomplete rotation outward of the arm as well as incomplete supination of the forearm. If the amount of mobility in the shoulder joint is normal, the tendency of the arms to move forward is usually overcome by a sufficiently vigorous contraction of the deltoid (especially its posterior and central portions), the trapezius, the rhomboids

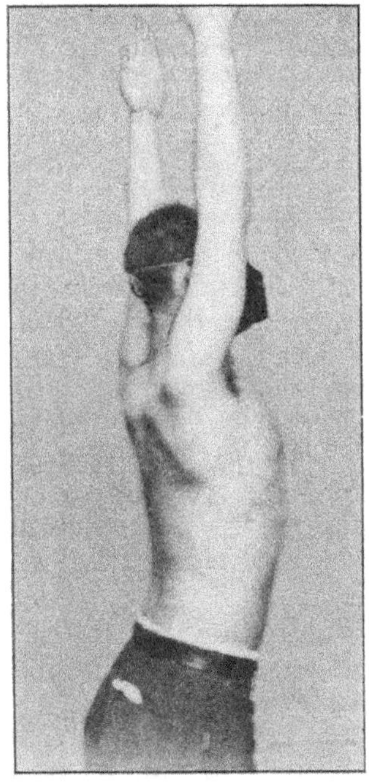

FIGURE 12

POSITION REACHED BY ARM RAISING SIDEWAYS-UPWARD OR FORWARD-UPWARD, OR ARM STRETCHING UPWARD

and the latissimus, while complete and intense contraction of the infraspinatus, teres minor and the supinators of the forearm are necessary to keep the palms turned toward each other. When mobility is limited on account of shortness of the muscles and fibrous structures in front, so that the arms cannot be brought to the vertical position, shoulder distance apart, the expedient of bending backward in the lumbar spine is often resorted to (usually quite unconsciously), thereby obtaining an appearance of correct position at the end of the movement. This is of course to be discouraged. A more acceptable terminal position in such cases is one with the arms in the transverse plane of the body, but directed more or less obliquely outward and upward, perhaps allowing the elbows to bend a little so that the hands are not much more than shoulder distance apart. This insures complete contraction of the posterior muscles, while subjecting the resistant structures to as much tension as the individual can, or cares to, exert. At the same time he is not deceived into thinking that he is doing one movement while he is really doing another, and one which he is better off without. When the correct terminal position is obtained the strong tension on the pectorals and latissimus, as well as on the lower serratus (which is also in a state of complete contraction), exerts a correspondingly vigorous pull on the ribs to which these muscles are attached. A very marked chest expansion is the result.

The return to the fundamental position (arms straight, moving through the side plane) is accomplished by gravity, the muscles which produced the first movement now being the antagonistic force, remaining in a state of "eccentric" contraction and so regulating the speed of the return movement. The steadying muscles are the same as before, while the former antagonistic muscles (adductors and rotators inward of the shoulder joint and rotators downward of the scapula) now aid gravity by their increased action, especially if the return movement is a quick one.

13. *Arm raising forward to the horizontal position.* The hands are kept at shoulder distance. The movement is principally a flexion in the shoulder joint, but includes also a certain amount of displacement of the shoulder girdle. This displacement varies in kind and amount according to the habitual position of the scapula and upper back, the shape of the chest, and the amount of muscular control possessed by the individual. Ordinarily, the whole scapula moves away from the mid-spinal line—is abducted; its lower angle swings outward and forward; and the plane of the scapula is changed from one approximately parallel with the back to one more nearly approaching the sagittal plane of the body. At the same time the vertebral scapular border is brought

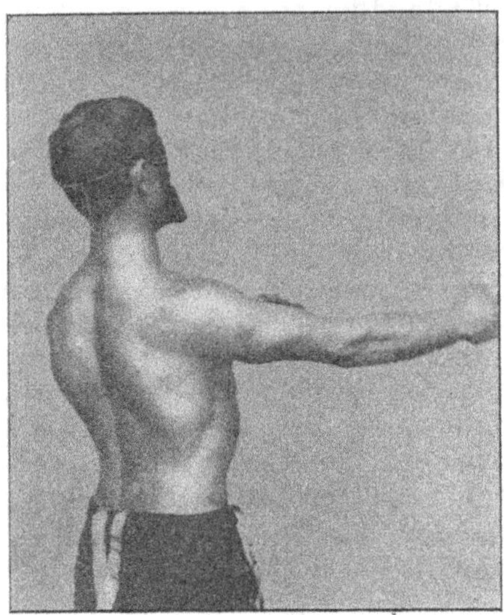

FIGURE 13

POSITION REACHED BY ARM RAISING FORWARD, OR ARM STRETCHING FORWARD

away from the back and may be seen or felt sharply projecting under the skin. In other words, the scapula revolves around its longitudinal axis and also swings outward, pendulum fashion, by a gliding movement in the acromio-clavicular joint, while at the same time the outer end of the clavicle travels forward by a movement in the sternal-clavicular joint. The displacement of the scapula is therefore neither a true rotation upward nor a simple abduction in the senses in which these terms are ordinarily used.

The muscles producing the flexion in the shoulder joint are the anterior portion of the deltoid and the upper (clavicular) portion of the pectoralis major, aided by the short (and long) head of the biceps and the coraco-brachialis. The displacements of the shoulder girdle forward are partly due to the passive tension of the teres major and minor which always occurs when the arm moves away from the body; partly to the contraction of the serratus magnus especially its lower and middle portions, as well as of the lower and middle trapezius (Mollier). If the movement is vigorous and quick and especially if the effort is made to reach as far forward as possible, the whole pectoralis major and the whole serratus are active. The pectoralis minor and the leva-

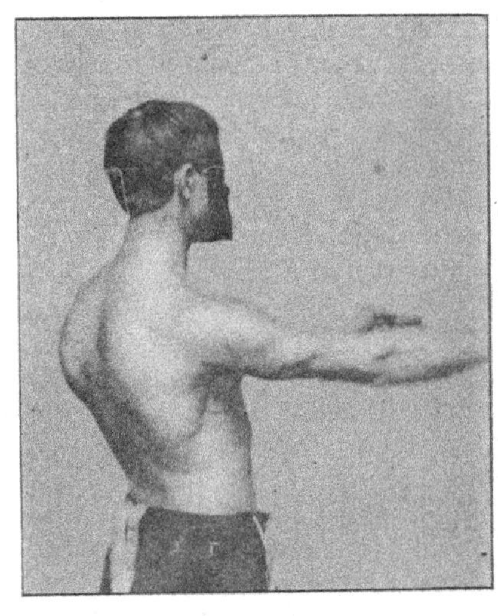

FIGURE 14

FAULTY ARM RAISING FORWARD

tor anguli scapulæ are probably also then associated with the other muscles.

So far what might be called the "non-gymnastic" type of the movement has been described. For certain reasons already alluded to under "Forward bending of arms" (see page 33) it is not desirable to do movements in this way in gymnastic practice. Here our object should be to avoid as much as possible displacements of the shoulder girdle. In the exercises so far analyzed the fixations of the scapula were (1) in connection with rotation outward in the shoulder joint, as in "Arm bending," where the effort to resist the rotation upward of the scapula associated with abduction of the arm was the chief feature; (2) in connection with simple abduction of the arm as in "Arm raising sideways" and in "Forward bending of arms," demanding conscious effort to resist abduction, elevation and excessive rotation upward of the scapula; (3) in connection with combined abduction and rotation outward in the shoulder joint, occurring in "Arm raising sideways with palms up," in "Half sideways bending of arms" and in "Placing hands behind neck," requiring even greater effort to resist the tendency to elevation, abduction and rotation upward of the scapula, associated and partly replaced in the last-named movement with special effort to keep the head in the fundamental position. In "Arm raising forward" the displacements of the shoulder girdle described above are frequently excessive and obviously of a very undesirable kind, strongly tending to emphasize faulty structural relations and to encourage or confirm "vicious" motor habits in this region. For these reasons the first definition of the movement should be qualified by requiring that the scapular displacements be reduced to a minimum. This at once changes the character of the movement from an easy, natural one to an exercise of considerable difficulty and hard work. It brings into action all the scapular adductors, and as they work in opposition to the direction of the main movement, a considerable amount of coördination, as well as vigorous contraction, is required to enable them to maintain a fair degree of fixation of the scapula. They are also at a mechanical disadvantage, particularly as compared with the indirect abductor of the scapula, the pectoralis major. Although only the clavicular portion of the latter contracts when the movement is done slowly and easily, the whole muscle is active whenever a quick or forcible movement is attempted, and especially when the hands are brought nearer together than shoulder distance. This is apt to be the case unless guarded against. By successful management of the scapular adductors, the terminal position is changed from one with more or less rounded back and depressed chest to one with relatively straight, flat back and moderately expanded chest, results which always accompany the proper interplay of the scapular fixators.

Because the problem in coördination offered in this exercise is one of some difficulty, it is wisest not to introduce it too early in gymnastic training, but to wait until a fair degree of control of the scapular muscles has been acquired by the practice of some of the easier shoulder blade exercises, in which the movement of the arms, and therefore the action of the shoulder joint muscles, is less in opposition to the action of the scapular adductors and depressors.

14. *Arm parting,* following "Arm raising forward." From the horizontal position in front the arms are moved directly backward in the horizontal plane. The palms may be turned down or up. Anatomically this is equivalent to abduction and extension in the shoulder joint, with adduction of the scapula, and slight rotation inward or complete rotation outward in the shoulder joint according as the palms are turned down or up. The former will be assumed in this case. The motor muscles are the deltoid, the trapezius, especially its central portion, aided by the rhomboids. The terminal position is the same as that reached by "Arm raising sideways." The same difficulties are encountered here, viz., the tendency of the shoulders to rise and of the arms to droop. This is particularly marked if the movement is quick or the resistance increased by chest weights, dumb bells, etc. Under such conditions special effort is also needed to keep the head and neck from moving forward and the lower back from excessive arching. This, it will be readily seen, is equivalent to a bending of the upper back. •By allowing this to happen, one of the main objects of the movement—improving the posture in this region—is defeated, it being one of the most commonly used and typical "setting-up" exercises.

The muscles whose vigorous contraction is necessary for the proper execution of the movement are the scapular depressors, notably the lower trapezius and the latissimus, the posterior neck and abdominal muscles. Because of the difficulty of properly coördinating the action of all these muscles (described at length under "Forward bending of arms"), it is best to practice the movement slowly at first, and with little or no weights in the hands.

The return movement is accomplished by the contraction of the anterior deltoid, the serratus magnus (lower and central portions) and the pectoralis major (chiefly the upper portion). The difficulties here, and the secondary muscular action called for in overcoming them, are similar to those described in "Arm raising forward."

15. *Arm raising forward-upward.* Having reached the hori-

zontal position in front, as described in "Arm raising forward," the continuation of the movement upward to the vertical position—arms straight overhead, palms facing each other—brings about a position of the joints identical with that obtained by "Arm raising sideways-upward," viz., complete abduction and rotation outward in the shoulder joint, complete rotation upward of the scapula and complete supination of the forearm. That the changes of position in the shoulder joint, occurring gradually as the movement proceeds, are really a blending of those which are termed abduction and rotation outward when started from the fundamental position of this joint, plus a rotation upward of the scapula, may perhaps be more readily understood if the component elements of the movement are imagined, for the sake of illustration, to occur one at a time in a certain sequence. Assume for the moment that "Arm raising forward" is a pure flexion of ninety degrees in the shoulder joint (with a few degrees of rotation outward), the scapula remaining immovable. Now move the arm backward as in "Arm parting." That brings the shoulder joint into a position of complete abduction and *extension*. Next turn the palms up. This involves complete rotation outward in the shoulder joint and complete supination of the forearm. Finally, rotate the scapula upward on its central (horizontal) axis, and (with a little additional abduction in the shoulder joint) the vertical position of the arms with the palms turned inward is reached.* The real movement is simply a "short-cut," and its different elements take place gradually and simultaneously. The abduction and rotation of the scapula on its length axis occurring when the movement passes through the horizontal position (see "Arm raising forward") are somewhat reversed during the last stage, as the arm is forced into the vertical position.

The active muscles during the last half of the movement (from the horizontal to the vertical) are (1) the posterior and central deltoid, which, aided by the active resistance of the latissimus and teres major, accomplishes the backward movement of the arm in the shoulder joint (corresponding to abduction and extension), and also contributes to the rotation outward in this joint; (2) the infraspinatus and teres minor, which are chiefly responsible for this rotation outward; (3) the trapezius, whose vigorous contraction, aided by the continued action of the serratus, completes the rotation upward of the scapula; and (4) the rhomboids (and levator anguli scapulæ), which, while antagonistic to the rotation upward, help the trapezius to adduct the scapula and

---

*An absolutely vertical position of the *upper* arm is probably only obtained by individuals with exceptionally free mobility in the joints of the shoulder girdle. Mollier is of the opinion that it never occurs without compensatory trunk movements.

to press it into closer apposition to the back.  In this, during the final stage of the movement, they are associated with and aided by the latissimus through its pull on the arm in a backward-inward (as well as downward) direction.

Here, as in "Arm raising sideways-upward," the resistance due to stretching of ligaments and antagonistic muscles increases rapidly during the last stage of the movement.  Limitations of mobility on this account, or insufficient effort on the part of the motor muscles, are shown by the same faulty or incomplete terminal position as was described in "Arm raising sideways-upward."  Compensatory backward bending in the lumbar spine is here even more marked, especially if the movement is done quickly, or with weights in the hands.  But by doing it quickly (without weights) and taking particular care not to hyperextend the lower back, the resistant anterior structures may be subjected to an even more forcible stretching than in "Arm raising sideways-upward."

The return movement, if slow, is accomplished by gravity, the former motor and steadying muscles still remaining in a state of contraction (eccentric) to check the speed and determine the plane of the movement.  If the latter is done quickly, the former antagonistic muscles—latissimus, teres major, pectoralis major, subscapularis and the rotators downward of the scapula, principally the rhomboids and pectoralis minor—contract with greater vigor, while the deltoid, supraspinatus, infraspinatus, teres minor, trapezius and serratus relax more or less.  As it is usually desired to work the latter set as much as possible, and at the same time to stretch the pectorals and anterior ligaments of the shoulder joint, the return to the fundamental position is better done through the side plane (sideways-downward).  The whole movement is then what is called *"Arm Circumduction"* or "Arm Circling."

16. *Arm stretching upward,* following "Arm bending."  This, too, brings the arms to the same terminal position as does "Arm raising sideways-upward," viz., with the shoulder joint in a position of complete abduction and rotation outward, the scapula completely rotated upward and the forearm supinated.  Starting, however, from the position reached by "Arm bending," the complete outward rotation in the shoulder joint and the supination of the forearm have already taken place.  "Arm stretching upward" involves then, further, complete abduction in the shoulder joint, complete rotation upward of the scapula, and extension of the elbow.  The muscles concerned in this are the same as those responsible for the same elements of "Arm raising sideways-upward"—the deltoid and supraspinatus (and biceps), the trapezius and serratus magnus—as well as the triceps.  The rhom-

boids, although antagonistic to the upward rotary action of the trapezius, by their adduction of the scapula contribute an important share in the effort to keep the arm moving through or behind the lateral plane of the body, and in keeping it well back in the terminal position. The deltoid is also responsible for this, and must contract with utmost vigor to accomplish it. In this effort to keep the arm back the active resistance offered by the latissimus may also help during the last stage of the movement. The return movement of·"Arm bending" from the position with arms overhead, whether quick or slow, involves powerful and complete contraction of the adductors of the shoulder joint—latissimus, teres major, pectoralis major and the long head of the triceps; the rotators downward of the scapula—rhomboids (levator anguli scapulæ) and pectoralis minor; and the flexors of the elbow—biceps and brachialis anticus. The rotators outward of the shoulder joint should remain in a state of complete contraction, while the now antagonistic abductors of the shoulder joint, and rotators upward of the scapula contract "eccentrically" more or less according to the speed of the movement.

17. *Arm stretching sideways,* following "Arm bending." This is like "Arm raising sideways," except that, starting from a position with the arms rotated outward and the elbow flexed, there is, in addition, rotation inward in the shoulder joint and extension in the elbow joint. This means action of the corresponding muscles added to the muscular mechanism of "Arm raising sideways." Otherwise, the action of motor, steadying and fixator muscles is the same as described under that movement (see page 30).

The return movement is in all respects similar to that already described under "Arm bending" from the fundamental position.

18. *Arm stretching forward,* following "Arm bending" is like "Arm raising forward," plus rotation inward in the shoulder joint and extension in the elbow joint with the corresponding muscular action.

The return movement is practically the same as "Arm bending" from the fundamental position.

19. *Arm stretching backward,* following "Arm bending." The hands are thrust downward and as far backward as possible *without disturbing the position of the chest, shoulders and back.* It involves, therefore, rotation inward and hyperextension in the shoulder joint. The motor muscles are the latissimus dorsi, teres major, subscapularis (pectoralis major and the anterior deltoid). As the amount of hyperextension in the shoulder joint is very limited, the arm cannot go far behind the plane of the back without displacement of the scapula. When the movement is done

vigorously, this is extremely likely to happen, unless guarded against by emphatic admonitions. The displacement of the scapula referred to is of a particularly undesirable kind. It is an elevation, combined with complete rotation downward and, besides, a tilting of the bone so that its upper border moves forward, causing the point of the shoulder to project, while its lower angle moves backward and protrudes markedly under the skin. This displacement is caused by the excessive action of the latissimus in its effort to produce hyperextension combined with rotation inward in the shoulder joint. The coraco-humeral ligament and anterior part of the capsule are soon tense, and further action of the latissimus, with good leverage through the arm, pries the scapula into the tilted position described above. This is made more pronounced by the associated action of the levator anguli scapulæ, which pulls the upper end of the bone somewhat forward as well as upward. It also rotates the scapula downward. There is probably also induced contraction of the other rotators downward of the scapula—rhomboids and pectoralis minor. The action of the latter tends to make the tilting more pronounced.

To check this tendency to scapular displacements, the trapezius and the serratus magnus (lower and middle) must contract powerfully. When this is done the movement may be as quick and energetic as the individual is able to make it. Because of the peculiar antagonistic and forcible action of the latissimus, serratus and pectorals, all of which are attached to the ribs, the chest expansion is very extreme in this exercise, providing it is properly done.

The distinctive feature of all the arm stretchings in the different directions, preceded by arm bending, is that they are capable of being done with great speed and vigor. This favors correct execution by calling for more initial intensity of the muscular contractions, and by forcibly stretching the resistant structures through the very momentum of the moving arm. This, in turn, is helpful in insuring completeness of movement in the joints. To make it count for as much as possible the terminal positions should be held for at least a brief space of time. Otherwise the recoil of the ligaments and muscles whose resistance has been overcome would tend to make the movements oscillatory in character, with all the loss of effectiveness that this implies. To avoid such rebound with accompanying muscular relaxation, it is of advantage to make the rhythm uneven by doing the stretching movement faster than the bending, and by holding the terminal position reached by the former slightly longer than that reached by the latter.

### B.  SUSPENSION EXERCISES.

**20.  *The Hanging Position.*** When the body is suspended on the arms the joints of the shoulder girdle and arm remain in the positions reached by "Arm raising" or "Arm stretching upward," viz., complete abduction and rotation outward in the shoulder joint, complete rotation upward of the scapula and complete supination of the forearm.  But here gravity, instead of muscular contraction, maintains these positions of the joints.

In what may be called the *relaxed hanging position,* the weight of the whole body, with the exception of the arms, is passively suspended on the ligaments and muscles which were antagonistic in "Arm raising" or "Arm stretching upward;" principally the pectorals, subscapularis, latissimus, teres major and the rhomboids.  All these are subjected to strong tension, and on their relative length, tone and extensibility will depend the amount of chest expansion and straightening of the back produced.  When these muscles and ligaments are short, and mobility in the joints of the shoulder girdle and upper spine limited, the posture of the back and chest may not be influenced as much as might be expected or desired.  Of course frequent and prolonged passive suspension will in time stretch the resistant structures somewhat and so make possible a better hanging as well as standing position.

In what we will call the *active hanging position,* the tension on the resistant structures is increased by effort on the part of the individual to "throw out his chest."  This involves here, as always, contraction of the scapular adductors and depressors.  The lower and middle trapezius and rhomboids act most directly and effectively in this effort.  The latissimus and the posterior and central portions of the deltoid also aid powerfully, the immediate purpose of their contraction being to bring the arms and trunk into line.  As the arms cannot move backward, the trunk must move forward and upward between the shoulders, so to speak.  This is simply another way of describing adduction in the shoulder joint, adduction, depression and slight rotation downward of the scapula.  As this bone cannot really move much in this position, the arms being fixed, the trunk is here the moving segment.  Any forward-upward movement of the trunk means chest expansion, providing the back is kept straight.  This is done by the contraction of the erector spinæ group, which is usually, if not always, associated with vigorous contraction of the scapular adductors and depressors.  When the action of all these muscles is very strong, there is apt to be an excessive arching of the

---

*In order to avoid too much detail it will be assumed that the position is taken on some such apparatus as the suspended parallel bars, with hands facing each other.

lower back and sometimes a slight adduction in the shoulder joint (spreading of the arms), flexion in the elbow and some real rotation downward of the scapula. Any or all of these effects may be chiefly due to the excessive action of the latissimus dorsi and erector spinæ, but are probably contributed to by the combined action of all the muscles enumerated, as well as by irresistible associated contraction of the pectorals and biceps. When the last three are innervated sufficiently, arm bending or "pull up" is the result. The execssive arching of the back is difficult to eliminate, as the muscular action necessary for this must now take place under conditions of fixation entirely different from normal, and largely the reverse. Any effort to straighten the hollow in the lower back usually leads to a general rounding of the whole back and raising of the legs. The reason for this is the difficulty, considerable even in the standing position, of dissociating the action of the abdominal muscles from that of the pectorals and hip joint flexors under these changed conditions of fixation. This matter will be further discussed under "Arm bending from the hanging position."

The value of the "hanging position" as a gymnastic exercise depends then on the degree to which it is "active" in the sense described above. The distance between the hands is important in this connection. For the well-built individual shoulder distance will do, but it is better to have more than less. The position with the hands close together usually means here, as in "Arm raising and stretching upward," a failure to bring the arms and trunk into line, that is, insufficient straightening of the back and incomplete chest expansion to compensate for the (then artificially) limited range of motion in the joints of the shoulder girdle. The spreading of the arms allows them to move further backward, or, what is the same thing, allows the trunk to move further forward, by the contraction of the scapular adductors, latissimus and deltoid. These muscles are now working with better mechanical advantage, less obliquity and greater leverage, while the pectorals do not profit correspondingly by increasing the distance between the arms. For what they gain in these respects in the lateral plane by the spreading of the arms is more than neutralized by their increased obliquity and diminished leverage in the antero-posterior plane by the relatively more posterior position of the arms. In fact, the chief effect of this on the pectorals is to maintain and even increase their tension, thereby enhancing the general chest expansion, which is already considerable owing to the pull of the latissimus, the stretching of the lower serratus and the strong contraction of the longitudinal back muscles.

At the same time, by increasing the distance between the hands, the weight leverage increases relatively more than the muscular leverage. This, together with the better opportunity for work offered the trapezius, deltoid, latissimus and rhomboids, and the undiminished static (or even eccentric) contraction of the pectorals, tends to make the position with the hands far apart decidedly "active."

21. *Suspension exercises derived from or similar to the hanging position.* What has been said regarding the hanging position applies equally to exercises derived from it, such as *hand traveling* forward, backward and sideways, with straight arms, on the ladders, suspended parallel bars, boom, etc.; or variations such as swinging and traveling on the rings; or suspension exercises with additions such as knee-upward bending and leg raising. In the last named the additional elements involve the joints and muscles of the lower trunk and will again be referred to.

In hand traveling the weight of the whole body is suspended a varying length of time on one arm. When this period is of brief duration, as in straight, forward or backward traveling by very short "steps" on the horizontal ladder or suspended parallel bars, there is only a slight difference from the "hanging position," chiefly one of degree, in the action of the muscles concerned. This may, in the case of individuals with relatively weak shoulder and trunk muscles and considerable weight, be enough to preclude success. The scapular muscles on the supporting side in conjunction with the abdominal and back muscles on the opposite side are then not able to hold the body rigid long enough, nor to give it sufficient twist (which is chiefly a rotation outward or inward in the shoulder joint of the supporting side) to allow the released hand to be shifted.

In traveling on the rings the body is in what we have called the relaxed hanging position, on one arm, the greater part of the swinging period, with nearly complete rotation upward, elevation and especially abduction of the scapula, as well as abduction in the shoulder joint. The successful grasping of the next ring depends partly on the skillful management of momentum (including the twist), gained in releasing the last ring, partly on a sufficiently powerful and well-timed effort to produce rotation outward in the shoulder joint of the supporting side (if the turn is forward, inward if the turn is backward). This is combined with a rising movement of the trunk, corresponding to a slight rotation upward of the scapula on the same side. There is also some real twisting of the trunk towards this side. The latter is sometimes aided by a scissors-like movement with the legs to furnish the necessary momentum.

Rotary traveling forward or backward on ladder, bars or boom is practically identical with traveling on the rings, except that the swinging period is briefer.

All exercises of the character indicated by the examples given are extremely valuable for improving the posture of the upper part of the body, for increasing the mobility of the chest and training the mechanical part of the respiratory organs, as well as for strengthening and developing the musculature of the upper trunk, shoulders and arms. They require comparatively little skill and include types easy enough for the weakest. To produce the greatest benefit they must, however, be done with due regard to good form, i.e., posture, and be of the "active" rather than the "relaxed" variety.

22. *Arm bending from the hanging position.* As in "Arm bending" from the fundamental standing position, there are many variations of this movement, e.g., with reverse grasp, ordinary (over) grasp, combined grasp; with elbows moving forward, or more or less sideways; hands close together or far apart. The most common is the familiar "pull-up" or "chinning the bar," usually done with the reverse grasp, sometimes with one hand on each side of the bar, generally with the hands less than shoulder distance apart, and always with elbows moving forward. The reverse grasp will be assumed in analyzing the movement.

In the hanging position with the reverse grasp, the weight of the body may be said to be suspended on the (flexors and) extensors, adductors and rotators inward of the shoulder joint, the adductors, depressors and rotators downward of the scapula, and the flexors of the elbow. When the tone of these muscles is good, the ligaments are not called upon to bear much weight, unless the body is suddenly dropped into this position. The reverse grasp demands more twisting of the arm than can be met by even the most extreme rotation outward in the shoulder joint and supination of the forearm. This necessitates a supplementary adjustment of the humerus, scapula and trunk, relative to each other, equivalent to a small amount of flexion in the shoulder joint (moving the arms forward-downward) with a forced abduction and rotation upward of the scapula, as well as a tilting of this bone, bringing it to a position on the side and top of the chest, with its lower angle projecting in the posterior axilla. This adjustment is caused in the first instance by the forcible stretching of the pectoralis major, subscapularis and teres major, all producing rotation inward in the shoulder joint, and by their tension checking rotation outward.

*Arm bending from this position, with the elbows moving forward,* is a flexion in the elbow, partial flexion, followed by extension and rotation inward in the shoulder joint, and a rotation downward with incomplete adduction and depression of the scapula. The muscles which bring about the movement are the pectoralis major and minor, the subscapularis, the latissimus dorsi and teres major, the rhomboids, biceps and brachialis anticus.

The extreme abduction of the scapula induced by the reverse grasp places the humèrus in such a position that the pull of the pectoralis major, latissimus, subscapularis and teres major will more readily move. it forward-downward than in any other direction. This plane of the movement offers the most favorable mechanical conditions—least obliquity and best leverage—for all the muscles, with the possible exception of the latissimus. This

FIGURE 16<br>
ARM BENDING FROM THE HANGING<br>
POSITION WITH REVERSE GRASP

works perhaps equally well when the arm moves in the lateral plane. The pectoralis minor, too, is able to work to best advantage with the scapula in this position of extreme abduction, its action being then most direct and effective in producing rotation downward of the scapula. Finally, the weight leverage increases at a less rapid rate when the arms move forward than is the case when they move in a more lateral plane. This reduction (or rather, least possible increase) of weight leverage is made possible by the forward movement of the lower part of the trunk and legs to compensate for the backward movement of the head, shoulders and upper trunk, thus keeping the weight of the body as a whole well under the points of support. The forward movement of the lower trunk is in part due to the pull of the latissimus, whose fibres run forward and upward when the arm moves forward, partly to the almost involuntary contraction of the abdominal muscles. This in turn induces contraction of the flexors of the hip joint, being at all times even more intimately associated, functionally, with the abdominal muscles than the latter are with the pectorals. The result of all this is not only to draw the body forward sufficiently to reduce the weight leverage to a minimum, but even to overdo it, by raising the legs forward. This necessitates displacement of an equal amount of weight backward, accomplished by extreme rounding of the upper back, with accompanying contraction of the chest. The last two features may, however, be somewhat obviated by conscious effort on the part of the individual to keep his chest expanded and to refrain from raising the legs. In any case, a better position of the back, chest and scapulæ may be obtained by keeping the hands far apart. But this also makes the exercise harder, because the elbows are not then moved forward as readily, and the mechanical conditions are less favorable (see below).

Another feature usually occurring in this exercise is the marked forward position of the head. It is partly a result of the backward convexity of the upper thoracic spine, partly due to the strong pull of the sterno-mastoid and the other anterior neck muscles, which, like the abdominal muscles, are closely associated with the pectorals. This fault is often exaggerated by the individual's desire to "chin" the bar in the traditionally approved style.

On account of the strong tendency to a poor position of the shoulder blades, chest, back and head in this form of the movement, it is of no value as a corrective exercise, if it does not, indeed, work the other way. But it is useful in developing and strengthening the chest and arm muscles, as it always involves complete and powerful contraction of these muscles. Because the resistance to be overcome—the whole body weight—is so great, relative to the size and leverage of the muscles, the latter are soon fatigued, and the average man can repeat the exercise only a comparatively small number of times, while the majority of women and many men cannot do it at all, although it is the easiest type of "Arm bending from the hanging position."

*Arm bending with ordinary grasp, elbows moving sideways.* When the exercise is done with the ordinary grasp—hands on the near side of the bar (overgrasp) and at least shoulder distance apart—there is not such extreme rotation outward in the shoulder joint with the resultant forced abduction of the scapula. The elbows do not tend to move as far forward as when the reverse grasp is used, although they can be made to do so by conscious effort. On the other hand, they can be more readily moved in or near the transverse plane of the body; but conscious effort is needed here, too.

This type of the exercise calls for vigorous action of the deltoid (posterior and central portions) and the latissimus dorsi reënforced by the associated contraction of the scapular adductors, trapezius and rhomboids. The scapula is thereby kept in good apposition to the back during its rotation downward, which, it will be remembered, is a part of the arm bending. This puts the pectoralis minor, one of the rotators downward of the scapula, at a its pull very oblique and somewhat "around the corner" (the side of mechanical disadvantage, making the upper chest). Thus a large part of its force is spent in traction on the ribs to which it is attached

FIGURE 17

ARM BENDING FROM THE HANGING POSITION WITH ORDINARY GRASP

(third, fourth and fifth), leading to their elevation. The lateral plane of the arm movement puts the pectoralis major, too, at a mechanical disadvantage, keeping the majority of its fibres very nearly in line with the humerus and close to the shoulder joint. Moreover, as the movement progresses, the weight leverage increases much more rapidly than the leverage of the latissimus, biceps, rhomboids and trapezius. Here the "curling up" of the trunk and legs is of no advantage. Because of this rapidly increasing weight leverage, in addition to the poor leverage and oblique pull of the pectorals, arm bending with the elbows moving in the side plane is a much harder exercise than arm bending with the reverse grasp and elbows moving forward. But on the other hand, the contraction of the pectorals, while not being of much help in the production of the movement, is an important factor in the forcible expansion of the upper chest. This, as well as straightening and flattening of the back, is a marked feature in this type of arm bending, because of the strong contraction of the scapular depressors and the longitudinal back muscles.

The unfavorable mechanical conditions in this type of arm bending make it more difficult and severe than any other. But these same conditions bring about the kind of muscular interplay which is most effective for purposes of postural improvement, namely, forcible stretching of the anterior ligaments and the pectorals—the latter being made very tense in their efforts to contract—and complete shortening against great resistance of the scapular adductors and posterior depressors and rotators downward. For purposes of developing the musculature of the upper trunk and extremity, this exercise is at least as effective as any type of arm bending. There is this drawback, however: being so hard to do, there are many people who have not the requisite strength to even attempt it. To acquire the strength, milder exercises with the same muscular mechanism may be practiced, such as arm bending with the overhead pulley weights; or modifications where a part of the weight is borne by the legs, such as "Arm stretching and bending with knee bending and stretching," done standing, with the bar, rings, ropes, etc., at the height of the chin; or arm bending from the "Fall hanging position," with the rigid body inclined more or less and supported in front on the heels (see below). Both of these exercises, while more complex in their mechanism and more general in their distribution of muscular work, are relatively easy as far as coördination is concerned. As regards the amount of local muscular work they may be graded to suit every individual.

23. *The Fall hanging position,* referred to above, involves the lower trunk and hip regions to a considerable extent. As regards the shoulder, the joints are in approximately the same positions as are reached by "Arm raising forward," viz., flexion in the shoulder joint, abduction, rotation upward and some elevation of the scapula. The arms being fixed, the trunk, held rigid by the longitudinal back muscles, tends to drop down between the shoulder blades. This is prevented by the latissimus and the scapular adductors, trapezius and rhomboids, together forming a sort of sling in which a part of the body weight is suspended. The other part is supported on the heels, the hip joint being kept extended by glutei and hamstring muscles.

Here, as in the "hanging position," the exercise may be more or less relaxed, involving merely passive tension on the above named muscles. It is then of little value. But it becomes a good corrective exercise when the proper muscular action—vigorous contraction of the adductors and depressors of the scapula and the upper prolongations of the erector spinæ—is induced by efforts to raise the chest and to throw the head back with "chin drawn in." It is also suitable as a preliminary to the more typical suspension exercises. This is even more true of the following.

24. *Arm bending from the Fall hanging position.* As in arm bending from the "hanging position" the elbows may move through any plane between the antero-posterior and the lateral.

When the elbows move forward there is extension in the shoulder joint, rotation downward with very little adduction of the scapula, and flexion in the elbow. The motor muscles are the pectorals, working with good leverage and decreasing obliquity; the lastissimus dorsi and teres major, also with favorable mechanical conditions; the rhomboids and trapezius, at a disadvantage and unable to produce much scapular adduction, having to contend against gravity as well as the more powerful and mechanically better favored pectorals. The biceps and other flexors of the elbow are of course also active. This is the easiest way to do the arm bending and, as usual when that is the case, the least favorable for good posture of the chest and back.

When the elbows move sideways there is a movement corresponding to abduction combined with extension in the shoulder joint, adduction with partial rotation downward of the scapula, and flexion in the elbow. There should also be conscious effort to depress the scapula, because the tendency here, as in "forward bending of arms," is to raise the shoulders, the muscular action being very much the same as in the latter movement. The deltoid and supraspinatus contract vigorously, as do also the latissimus, teres major, trapezius and rhomboids. The flexors of the elbow contribute their share, as in the preceding movement. The pectorals, however, are less active, and even if they contract, physiologically, they do not shorten much, if at all, and may even be somewhat stretched if the depression of the shoulders with the accompanying chest expansion is forcible enough.

25. *Climbing on the vertical ropes.* As far as the shoulder region is concerned the mechanism of this exercise is like that of "Arm bending from the hanging position" with the reverse grasp, hands close together and elbows moving forward. When properly done, the arms are relieved of a part of the weight during their bending by the simultaneous straightening of the legs, which have been previously drawn up and made to grasp the rope.

To favor a better position of the chest, shoulders and back, the exercise may be done on two ropes. This gives opportunity to move the arms in the side plane, because of the greater distance between the hands. With a little practice the leg grasp is not much more difficult than when a single rope is used. This modification of the exercise changes the muscular action in a way already described under "Arm bending from the hanging position" with overgrasp and hands far apart. When the ability has been acquired to shift the hands simultaneously and to hold, momentarily, an erect hanging position just before the legs are raised, the exercise has considerable corrective value, something the ordinary form of climbing, on one rope, lacks entirely.

26. *Starting the swing from the hanging position.* This is an excellent suspension movement in itself and is, besides, a necessary preliminary to many exercises on suspension apparatus. Like some of the preceding and following exercises, it involves, of course, more muscles and joints than those of the shoulder region and upper trunk, but the action of the latter only will be analyzed in detail.

The exercise may be described as consisting of three parts or phases, following each other without any appreciable pause. 1. The first is an ordinary arm bending, varying in degree according to the amount of swing desired. The mechanism of this has already been given. 2. Next the legs are raised, preferably with straight knees, by a flexion in the hips and lower back. This involves the flexors of the hip joint and the abdominal muscles. At the same time the arms are straightened, the head is thrown back, and the upper spine is extended or at any rate held rigid. This lowering of the head and shoulders with straightening of the elbows brings the shoulder joint in a position of partial flexion, with a partial rotation upward of the scapula. It serves to counterbalance the weight of the raised legs and lower trunk, and to deflect in a backward direction the more or less upward momentum acquired by their sudden elevation. At this moment, the trunk is in an approximately horizontal position. The muscles which were instrumental in producing the arm bending—the pectorals, latissimus, rhomboids and biceps—are all, with the exception of the latissimus, in a state of moderate static contraction. The same is true also of the upper and middle trapezius. The former, after their initial contraction, which raised the body to the bent arm hanging position, have yielded sufficiently to gravity and the pull of the latissimus to allow the upper part of the body to drop to this position. The latissimus, on the contrary, has contracted with increased intensity and has thereby been chiefly instrumental in raising the lower trunk almost to a level with the shoulders and head, the sudden drop of this portion of the body, acting as a counter-weight, having been the other factor. 3. The backward-upward momentum, attained in the first two parts of the exercise, is soon overcome by gravity. With the recoil, and the muscular efforts made to reënforce it, begins the third part of the exercise. This consists of a quick, partial bending, followed immediately by straightening of the elbow and a simultaneous extension in the hip joint, arching, or at least straightening of the lower back (previously flexed) and a forward projection of the whole body, now straight and rigid, which is equivalent to a forward-upward arm raising. This means additional flexion in the shoulder joint and rotation upward of the scapula. The muscles on whose well-timed and orderly response the successful execution of this part of the exercise depends are the hip and back extensors; the biceps and other elbow flexors; the upper pectoralis major and the anterior deltoid; the trapezius and serratus magnus. Their contraction must be quick and powerful and must cease promptly when the movement has progressed to a point where continued action would check the momentum gained. This is particularly true of the biceps, the upper pectoralis major and the anterior deltoid. As soon as the last two cease contracting, the central and posterior portions of the deltoid begin. The hip and back extensors remain contracted throughout to insure the necessary rigidity of the body as a whole.

The forward momentum gained in this way may be very considerable, even amounting to a forward-upward projection of the body. In any case, it is the principal force responsible for the completion of the flexion and the succeeding extension with abduction (i.e., the forward-upward movement of the arms) in the shoulder joint and the rotation upward with elevation, of the scapula, by which the arms and body are brought into line. At this point the body is in what might be called the "horizontal hanging position" and the starting of the swing has been accomplished.

The swing may be continued, pendulum-fashion, without further muscular effort until the momentum has been exhausted. Or the exercise may be finished by an immediate forward dismount simply by letting go with the hands and arching the back somewhat; or, by a dismount at the end of the first backward or the next forward swing; or other movements may be performed at the end of a forward or backward swing.

The exercise may be started by jumping, from behind the bar, to the bent arm hanging position. This serves the double purpose of facilitating the arm bending and furnishing additional forward momentum. It is of advantage when the muscular strength and control of the individual are inadequate for an effective start from the hanging position. It is also more suitable when it is desired to finish the exercise by an immediate forward dismount, when it is called the "swing jump" or "short underswing." The mechanism in this modification is essentially the same as that described above.

27. *Circling the bar to Front Rest. Return by forward circle.* Like the "starting of the swing," this exercise may be done from the hanging position, or it may be started by jumping, usually from behind the bar, to the bent arm hanging position. The latter method is the easier of the two, and will be assumed, especially as the former has already been described. To simplify analysis, the exercise may be considered as composed of four parts, as follows: 1. Jumping to the bent arm hanging position. This is in all respects like arm bending from hanging position, except that the momentum given by the jump lessens the resistance to be overcome by the working muscles—latissimus and teres major, pectorals, rhomboids and biceps. 2. Lowering the head and shoulders and at the same time raising the legs; the former

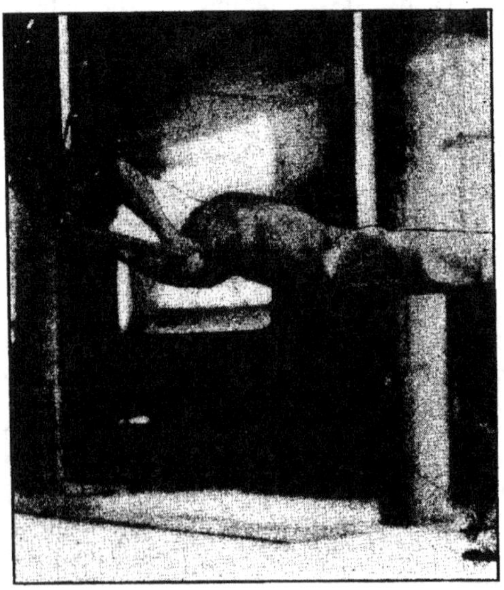

FIGURE 20

CIRCLING BAR TO FRONT REST.
FOURTH STAGE

by a straightening of the elbows and a slight forward movement of the arms, equivalent to a momentary partial flexion in the shoulder joint and a partial upward rotation, with abduction, of the scapula, followed immediately by the opposite movements; the latter by a bending at the hips, accompanied by more or less flexion in the lumbar and thoracic portions of the spine. All this must be done very quickly in order to attain sufficient momentum to carry the legs past the vertical. It is accomplished by the sudden contraction of the flexors of the hip joint, and the abdominal muscles in front; by the latissimus and teres major, upper erector spinæ and posterior neck muscles behind. The latter are, of course, aided by gravity. At the same time the pectorals, rhomboids and biceps, active during the first part of the exercise, yield momentarily to gravity and to the pull of the upper back muscles, contracting (eccentrically) only sufficiently to regulate the speed of the drop of the head and shoulders. When this has occurred they all, with the exception of the biceps, contract again for a moment to aid the latissimus and teres major in bringing the trunk to the vertical position, close to the arms. The body is now in the inverted hanging position, bent at the hips, the front of the thighs in contact with the bar. 3. If properly managed so far, the next stage of the exercise should begin immediately, before the momentum gained in the second part has been entirely spent. It consists of a quick arm bending, associated this time (owing to the inverted position of the body) with abduction in the shoulder joint and rotation upward with some elevation of the scapula. The motor muscles are, therefore, the biceps, the deltoid and supraspinatus; the trapezius and serratus magnus. The upper pectoralis major probably also helps, at least in the beginning. These muscles continue to contract until the body has been lifted high enough to bring the anterior spines of ilium opposite the bar. A partial flexion at the hips having been maintained, the legs have now passed the bar and are beginning to overbalance the trunk. This marks the beginning of 4, the last stage of the exercise. The body is now gradually straightened by contraction of the extensors of the hip joint and spine. Following closely, the elbows are also gradually straightened and the arms are brought to the sides. This is accomplished by reversing the muscular action in the shoulder region, the muscles active in the third stage relaxing, while the opposite set—latissimus and teres major, pectorals, rhomboids and triceps—are thrown into action. The trapezius (central and lower portions), however, should remain strongly contracted, to aid the rhomboids in keeping the scapula adducted. If these muscular efforts are well timed and are made in proper sequence, the now straight and rigid body revolves into a position of 45° inclination and is at the same time lifted until the front of the thighs rests on the bar and supports a part of the weight. If the momentum and balance are not skillfully managed—as by straightening the hips too soon, or too late, or too suddenly, or by waiting too long before beginning to straighten the elbows—there may be many a hitch in the proceedings, sometimes resulting in a return to the floor in reverse order, i.e., by an involuntary forward circle; or else the body, having begun to revolve, gathers too great momentum, passes the 45° angle and descends to the floor on the side of the bar from which the start was made, unless the performer has the strength to check it by a tardy, and therefore extreme, contraction of the extensors of hip, back, elbow and shoulder, and the rotators downward of the scapula.

*The return by a forward circle,* already mentioned as liable to occur involuntarily, before the final position on the bar has been reached, is started by a partial relaxation of the triceps, latissimus and teres major, pectorals and rhomboids. Gravity then causes the flexion in the elbow, abduction in the shoulder joint, and rotation upward of the scapula. As a result, the body is lowered until the hip joints are opposite the bar. At the same time, these joints are moderately flexed and the back slightly curved (the latter is not necessary, but is difficult to avoid). This is also caused by gravity, the hip and back extensors yielding sufficiently to allow it. If the flexion is not too great at first, the weight of the trunk now overbalances that of the legs and the body begins to revolve. Too great a momentum is guarded against by a further flexion at the hips, so that the front of the thighs remains in contact with the bar. The overturning of the trunk then takes place as follows: First, the trunk descends, head foremost, until

FIGURE 21

CIRCLING BAR TO FRONT REST. THIRD STAGE: OR, FORWARD CIRCLE FROM FRONT REST. SECOND STAGE the arms are straight; the biceps, deltoid, serratus and trapezius are actively resisting, but yielding to gravity sufficiently to check too sudden a drop.  Next, the hips are lowered, with continued flexion in order to keep the legs close to the bar, until the toes are opposite the latter.  This movement involves flexion in the shoulder joint (moving the arms forward-upward) and rotation upward of the scapula.  Gravity is the motor force, and the active muscles are those which resist the movement, viz., the extensors of the shoulder joint—pectoralis major, latissimus and teres major—and the rotators downward of the scapula—pectoralis minor and rhomboids.  While these contract "eccentrically" to control the speed of the movement, the abdominal muscles and hip joint flexors contract "concentrically" until the flexion at the hips and in the lower back is complete, thereby insuring the proximity of the legs to the bar throughout the descent and overturning of the trunk.  Finally, when the arms are straight and in line with the now vertical trunk, the legs are lowered by allowing the abdominal muscles and hip joint flexors to yield to gravity.  This continues until the hip joints are in complete extension and the back is straight, when the body is in the ordinary hanging position.

Variations in the manner of performing the forward circle are numerous.  The principal modification of the type described is the one in which the hips are straightened first, the elbows last.  This often occurs involuntarily, because of lack of strength and coördination on the part of the performer, but is also used by skillful gymnasts when other movements are to follow which require considerable swing or momentum.  The mechanism of this type of forward circle is practically the same as that described, except that the order of the different parts is changed.  Also, less effort is called for on the part of the abdominal muscles, and more on the part of the hip and back extensors, as well as on the shoulder joint extensors, the elbow and finger flexors and the rotators downward of the scapula in order to manage the much greater momentum.

28. *The inverted hanging position, and pull-up over bar to Back Rest.*  In the inverted hanging position the body is suspended vertically on the arms, head down.  The mechanism of the exercise varies somewhat with the apparatus used, and also according to minor details of definition.  Thus, when done between the parallel bars, ropes or rings the balance element is most pronounced and involves equal, or at any rate quickly alternating, action of the anterior and posterior shoulder, trunk and hip joint muscles.  When the horizontal bar or similar apparatus is used, the front of the thighs may be in contact with the bar, the position therefore demanding a more or less general muscular

action, but on the whole involving the anterior muscles slightly more than the posterior. This position is usually of a transitory character, occurring as a part of another exercise, e.g., circling the bar. Its main features have already been indicated. Or, the feet may be passed through between the hands, the legs then straightened, and the back slightly arched. The balance is then made easier through the support afforded by contact of the back of the thighs with the bar. The last-mentioned type will be assumed.

In taking the position the same muscular and joint action occurs as was described under "circling the bar," parts 1 and 2. Just before the legs reach the vertical the knees and hips are flexed sharply, to allow the feet to pass under the bar, between the hands. This flexion is produced by gravity, unless begun some time before the legs reach the vertical, when the hip joint flexors and abdominal muscles would be called into action. With this flexion is associated, as usual, marked curving of the whole back, the whole movement being fairly described by the term "curling up."

FIGURE 22

INVERTED HANGING POSITION

Next, the hip, knee and back extensors contract, producing complete straightening at the hips and knees, and a moderate arching of the back. This, if carefully done, brings the back of the thigh in contact with the bar. When the action of the back extensors is excessive, too great arching of the lower back is produced.

This, alone or combined with premature straightening of the knees, is liable to displace too much weight in the direction toward which the face is turned, and lead to an involuntary backward circle to the floor. To guard against this, or at any rate to minimize the arching of the lower back, the abdominal muscles have to maintain a moderate static contraction.

As regards the shoulder region, gravity is keeping the shoulder joint adducted or extended, and even slightly hyperextended.

The last is also due, in part at least, to the static contraction of the latissimus and teres major, associated with the back extensors (and gravity) in maintaining the arched position. The scapula is also kept rotated downward, adducted and depressed by gravity.

The position being decidedly "active," however, the weight is borne by the flexors and abductors of the shoulder joint—upper pectoralis major, deltoid and supraspinatus; the rotators upward of the scapula—middle trapezius and serratus; and the elevators of the scapula—upper trapezius, levator anguli scapulæ and the rhomboids. All these are in a state of moderate tonic contraction, while the lower trapezius, lower pectoralis major and the pectoralis minor are less active. The two latter are, however, subjected to strong tension.

When it is desired to *pull the body up over the bar* to the sitting position (or to the more active position of Back Rest), the above-named muscles contract more powerfully. They are joined by the biceps and brachialis anticus, while the latissimus and teres major relax more or less. This effort continues until the body has been raised sufficiently to bring the sacrum opposite the bar, when the weight of the legs overbalances that of the trunk (providing the extension in the hip joint and the arching of the back have been maintained). When this point has been passed, further contraction of these muscles must cease and muscular action of the opposite character begin, viz., contraction of the abdominal muscles and hip joint flexors; of the latissimus, teres major and triceps; and of the lower pectoralis major. The lower and middle trapezius, as well as the rhomboids, also contract, the latter with the double purpose of assisting the trapezius in keeping the scapula adducted and aiding the pectoralis minor in rotating it downward. As a result of these muscular efforts, the trunk, after passing the horizontal, is raised to the vertical position, or to a position with a backward inclination of about 45°, supported on the straight arms and the back of the thighs.

If the contractions of the muscles active during the "pull-up" do not cease at the right moment, the overbalance of the legs becomes too great, and the body is precipitated forward over the bar. If the final muscular efforts begin too soon, the body is liable to be pushed back, beyond the point of balance, and an involuntary backward circle to the floor is the result.

At all times during the last two stages of the movement, particular attention must be given to the position of the head. The tendency to bend it forward is very strong on account of the greater ease in balancing and guiding the movement when the performer is able to look up. Keeping the head forward also reduces the weight leverage of the trunk appreciably at the critical moment. After the point of balance has been passed, the forward position of the head is largely due to the close association of the anterior neck muscles with the pectoral and abdominal muscles which is particularly marked whenever the trunk is leaning back unsupported. For all these reasons it does not "come natural" to keep the head back. In fact, the necessary conscious effort to do so increases the difficulty of the exercise considerably.

29. *Upstart to Front Rest (the "Kip")*. This is one of the conventional modes of mounting the high bar. It is an exercise of no small difficulty, in spite of its apparent simplicity (when well done). This, and the fact that it is capable of being performed with a certain grace or style, make it a very popular exercise with young men, at once the never ending attraction and the despair of the uninitiated. Briefly considered, it may be said to consist of the following parts:

1. Starting the swing, as previously described. 2. On the next forward swing, the chest is forcibly expanded and the back arched as the body passes the vertical. This position is held, with absolute rigidity, until the forward swing is almost completed. The mechanism of this is practically identical with that of the "active" hanging position, already described. 3. A very small fraction of time before the forward swing is completed, the legs are quickly raised by a flexion in the hip joints. The less the spine is flexed, the better. 4. The legs are immediately brought down and back by a forcible extension in the hip joints and spine, while the arms, kept straight and rigid, are simultaneously pressed down to the sides, in other words, extension in the shoulder joint, rotation downward, depression and adduction of the scapula take place. The muscles concerned are the hip extensors and erector spinæ; the latissimus and teres major; the pectoralis major; the pectoralis minor and rhomboids; the lower trapezius; the triceps. It is on the proper timing, quickness and vigor of this complex muscular effort in relation to the recoil from the forward swing that the success of the exercise depends. If it is made a moment too soon or too late, if the extension at the hip is not complete, if the arching of the back is excessive, if the extension of the shoulder joint (the bearing down with the arms) is not strong enough, or if the elbows are allowed to bend before the body is vertical and its center of gravity above the level of the bar, the exercise becomes a futile, spasmodic, nondescript effort, the performer either striking the under side of the bar with his chest or abdomen or else swinging hopelessly backward and downward, instead of rising smoothly to the Front Rest position.

### C.  EXERCISES INVOLVING SUPPORT ON THE ARMS.

30. *Front Rest* (*Balance Weighing Position*).  This has already been mentioned and its mechanism indicated in connection with "Circling the bar" and "Upstart to Front Rest."  It may also be reached by a direct mount on any apparatus low enough to allow it; e.g., the low horizontal bar or boom, the horse or the buck.  Its definition may be briefly stated thus: body slightly arched, facing at right angle to the apparatus, inclined forward about 45 degrees, weight supported on the hands and upper part of the thighs.  It is used as a starting position for many exercises on the horizontal bar and horse, and in modified forms, without support on the thighs (variations of the so-called "Free" Front Rest), constitutes the principal transitory position of some vaults and dismounts on the horse, buck, low horizontal and parallel bars.

Although the body is in a position similar to the fundamental standing position, and the muscles responsible for the maintenance of the latter are here even more active, the relation of the muscular action to gravity is different. In the fundamental standing position gravity keeps the

FIGURE 23.  FRONT REST

elbow and shoulder joints in extension and the scapula rotated downward.  In "Front Rest," with a part of the weight supported on the arms, gravity tends to cause flexion in the elbow, abduction in the shoulder joint and rotation upward, with abduction and elevation of the scapula.  Gravity also helps to produce flexion at the hip and rounding of the back.  The last two features are apt to be pronounced when sudden and excessive efforts are made to regain the equilibrium, which at best is none too stable.

The active muscles are those which resist gravity, viz., the triceps; the adductors of the shoulder joint—latissimus and teres major, pectoralis major (lower portion); the rotators downward of scapula—pectoralis minor and rhomboids; the adductors and depressors of the scapula—trapezius (rhomboids, latissimus, pectoralis minor, already enumerated in other capacities); the extensors of the hip joint and back.

While the total amount of work performed by these muscles is considerable, the feature of particular interest in "Front Rest" is the difficulty it offers in maintaining good posture of the upper part of the body. This difficulty is related in the first place to the unstable equilibrium, in the second place to the large share of the work devolving on the pectorals in supporting the weight.

As regards the balance, it will readily be seen that the higher the body is raised above the bar and the greater its inclination, the more insecure is the position. For this reason the unskilled performer is reluctant to push up high enough to straighten the arms and to bring the upper part of the thighs into contact with the bar. Or, if he does so, he is apt to bend at the hips and at the same time to curve the back. This gives him a greater sense of security, because there is then less projection of weight on each side of the bar, with correspondingly lessened danger of acquiring too great momentum forward in attempts to find the point of balance.

Closely associated with this reluctance or inability to straighten the back for fear of becoming overbalanced is the excessive action of the pectorals and abdominal muscles. Indeed, it is the powerful action of the former which is chiefly responsible for the rounding of the upper back and the marked mal-position of the scapula, so common in this exercise; while the latter, in conjunction with the hip joint flexors (and gravity), cause the curving of the lower back and the bend at the hips. Attention has several times been called to the close functional association of all the anterior muscle groups, from the anterior neck muscles to the hip joint flexors. Whenever one set is very active one or all of the others are apt to be brought into play. This is especially true when the body is suspended or supported on the arms, the legs then being free to be moved in a way to balance displacements of weight in the upper part of the body. Illustrations of this occurred in the analysis of such exercises as "Arm bending from the hanging position," "Circling the bar," "Inverted hanging position." In "Front Rest" the tendency of the untrained individual is to try to escape the difficulties of balance involved in resting heavily on the thighs by supporting the greater part of the weight on the arms. This throws the largest share of the work on the pectorals. Their powerful contraction, aided by the associated action of the abdominal muscles, leads to a forward movement of the point of the shoulder and a rounding of the upper back. This is equivalent to a slight flexion in the shoulder joint and a marked displacement of the scapula by which this bone is not only abducted (moved away from the spine), but also tilted so that its lower angle projects sharply. The peculiar scapular displacement is due, primarily, to the excessive, unbalanced action of the pectoralis minor in its effort to prevent gravity from elevating and rotating the bone upward. While the projection forward of the point of the shoulder is due, largely, to this displacement of the shoulder girdle, it is made more pronounced by a simultaneous depression of the chest. The latter is bound to occur whenever the two large pectorals, acting as one muscle running over the convex surface of the upper chest, contract *completely*. They will then tend to get into a straight line. If the displacement of the shoulder girdle is not sufficient to allow this—as in the present case, the arms being fixed—the trunk will be forced backward. This can only mean curving of the thoracic spine and that, in turn, is always associated with depression and inversion of the ribs.

The prevention of this displacement of the shoulder girdle and the preservation of erect posture of the upper trunk devolve here, as always, on the scapular adductors and posterior depressors, aided by the longitudinal back muscles and hip joint extensors. Owing to the unusual difficulties encountered, as represented by the instability of the position, and the amount of weight to be supported on the arms with the consequent powerful action of the pectorals working with good leverage, the successful performance of this exercise demands, in the first place, fairly strong, well-developed upper back muscles. This is not infrequently lacking in those who attempt it. Secondly, the performer must have good control of the scapular muscles, as well as a fairly well-trained muscular sense generally, so that he is not inhibited too much by the difficulties of maintaining his equilibrium.

The practical application of all this to gymnastic teaching is to refrain from giving such an exercise to individuals who for one reason or another—youth, sex, untrained condition—have not the requisite strength and control to do it acceptably after a few attempts. Such individuals should receive preparatory training by practice of the various shoulder blade movements and simple suspension exercises already described, supplemented by such exercises as the "Prone falling position" and "Free Front Rest" (to be described).

When properly taken, however, the "Front Rest" position, by putting the muscles responsible for erect carriage of the upper trunk—the scapular depressors and adductors, the upper back and posterior neck muscles—to a most severe test, gives those muscles excellent training both as regards strength and control. It also cultivates in a high degree general muscular sense and coördination, the efforts to maintain the equilibrium involving more or less all the principal muscles in the body.

31. *"Free" Front Rest* is an exercise which may be used as a preparation for certain vaults and for "Front Rest," being somewhat similar to the latter in its mechanism. The term is really a misnomer, as the exercise is a movement rather than a position. For although the effort should be to hold it as long as possible, few are able to do so for more than a second, while the majority descend abruptly before having ascended even half way to the desired level. It may be described as a swinging up of the body toward the horizontal position, weight supported entirely on the arms. It is done on the horse, buck, low horizontal bar or boom, usually started by springing from the floor; or on the parallel bars preceded by a forward swing. In either case sufficient momentum is one of the necessary prerequisites for successful performance. Sufficient forward displacement of the weight is another. Strength is not as essential as might be supposed, provided full advantage is taken of the other two factors.

The body rises toward the horizontal position by a partial flexion in the shoulder joint and a partial rotation upward with some abduction of the scapula. The flexion in the shoulder joint is minimized by a compensatory hyperextension at the wrist involved in the projection of the head and upper trunk forward over the apparatus. By this means the arms are inclined forward so as to form a more acute angle with the trunk than would otherwise be the case, and the weight of the body as a whole is more evenly distributed in front and behind the support (the hands). The head and upper trunk thus act as a counterweight to the legs, and this, together with the momentum from the spring, makes possible the elevation of the body by the comparatively small motor muscles, working under adverse mechanical conditions. The muscles in question are the flexors of the shoulder joint—upper pectoralis major, anterior deltoid, biceps and coraco-brachialis; the rotators upward of the scapula—trapezius and serratus magnus (see below) ; and the extensors of the spine and hip.

The muscular mechanism is, however, not as simple as might be supposed from the above enumeration of the motor muscles. In the first place the triceps has to maintain a powerful contraction throughout to keep the elbow from bending too much under the weight. Similarly the lower pectoralis major, as well as the long head of triceps, must be kept strongly active to prevent gravity from producing abduction in the shoulder joint. This is especially true during the first part of the movement when the body is nearer the vertical than the horizontal position. Secondly, during the early stage of the movement the action of the trapezius and serratus should be confined to the lower portions of these muscles in the effort to resist the tendency of gravity to produce scapular elevation. When the horizontal plane is approached, however, these muscles are brought into full action, not so much to produce rotation upward of the scapula, although that inevitably occurs more than is desirable, but to aid in the proper fixation of the shoulder girdle.

At this point the whole body weight may be said to be suspended on the pectorals, major and minor, and the serratus on each side. These contract with utmost vigor to prevent the trunk from sinking down between the arms. This would lead to adduction and rotation downward of the scapula and to a bodily backward displacement of this bone. In their violent efforts to prevent this, the pectorals and serratus are apt to bring about the opposite condition, namely, extreme scapular abduction. That necessitates contraction of the scapular adductors, chiefly the trapezius and rhomboids, although the latissimus and levator anguli scapulæ are probably also active. Only in this way is the proper fixation of the shoulder girdle insured. The net results, under the most favorable conditions, of this interplay of the scapular muscles—abductors against adductors, elevators against depressors, rotators upward against rotators downward—plus the action of gravity, is a moderate rotation upward with some abduction and elevation of the scapula, while the upper back is kept straight and the chest moderately expanded by the upper prolongations of the erector spinæ and the deep back muscles.

When the exercise is first attempted there is usually only a very slight rise and even less incline of the body. The mechanism is then much like that of "Front rest," but the muscular work is easier because of the momentary character of the effort and the reduction in resistance represented by the momentum from the spring.

*32. Face vault (Front vault).* This is one of the horizontal vaults, in which the front of the body is toward the apparatus at the moment of passing it. It is a modification of "Free Front Rest" involving a 90-degree turn of the body at the moment of the spring, and a lateral movement of the legs and lower trunk, during the ascent as well as the descent, by means of which the landing is made on the other side of the apparatus. The mechanism is practically the same as that of "Free Front Rest," the principal differences being the slight excess of action of the back muscles on the side toward which the vault is made (e.g., the left), a transfer of the weight to the arm of the opposite side (right) and abduction combined with extension in the shoulder joint of that side during the last part of the movement. The difficulty here, as in "Free Front Rest," is to get enough momentum in the take-off, and to have enough weight in front of the hands during the progress of the movement to counterbalance the weight of the legs and lower trunk, thereby reducing the work of the motor muscles.  Partial failure in these respects shows itself by too large an angle between the arms and the body, and in landing a varying distance behind the hand which remains on the apparatus.  Another fault, peculiar to this exercise, is the tardy transfer of the weight to the arm on the side opposite that toward which the vault is made (right arm if the vault is to left), accompanied by too long retention of the hold of the other hand (left in this case) on the apparatus.  This leads to an excessive turn of the body in the same direction as the initial turn (right in this case) and a poor landing.

The placing of the hands is of some importance.  If the vault is made on the horse or buck, to the left, one hand on each side of the right end of the apparatus gives the best support; if the low horizontal bar is used the combined grasp is the most satisfactory.  Finally, the tendency here, as in crude attempts at "Free Front Rest," is to flex the knees, hips and back—curling up; this being the readiest and therefore the instinctive way of reducing the weight leverage.

33.  *Side vault (Flank vault)* is another of the horizontal vaults.  Here the side of the body is toward the apparatus at the moment of passing.  If the vault is to the left, the weight is transferred to the right arm immediately after the take-off, the left arm being used only momentarily to deflect to the right a part of the forward momentum of the upper trunk gained in the spring from the floor.  The success of the vault depends, as in the "Face vault," on sufficient momentum and proper distribution of the weight rather than on great strength.  The main features of the mechanism are as follows: The legs are raised to the left by a slight bend at the waist and by abduction in the right shoulder joint with rotation upward, abduction and slight elevation of the right scapula.  The displacement of the body to the right in the effort to distribute the weight more evenly over the right hand usually causes a slight bending of the right elbow, followed either immediately or in the last part of the vault by straightening of this joint.  The resulting inclination of the arm to the right reduces somewhat the extent of the above-mentioned shoulder joint and scapular movements.  The principal muscles active so far are the abdominal and lower back muscles of the left side; the left and right pectoralis major and minor, rhomboids and triceps for a moment only; then the right deltoid and supraspinatus, trapezius and serratus.  The right triceps yields a little as the legs are ascending and the weight is being shifted to the right arm.

When the legs have reached the highest point and the body as a whole is in an approximately horizontal position directly over the apparatus, the bend to the left in the waist and the slight flexion of the hip joints that may have occurred during the ascent are suddenly eliminated and the whole back extended by the vigorous contraction of the longitudinal back muscles and the hip joint extensors. The deltoid and supraspinatus, trapezius and serratus on the right side, active during the ascent, are at this moment making their most vigorous effort, the initial momentum being almost spent and what remains being utilized to carry the body past the apparatus.

The descent of the legs and the return of the body to the vertical are accomplished partly by gravity, partly by a quick, vigorous contraction of the right triceps, latissimus, teres major, pectorals, rhomboids and lower trapezius, resulting in a straightening of the elbow, previously slightly bent, adduction with hyperextension of the arm and rotation downward with depression of the scapula. The whole muscular effort is in the nature of a spring from the right arm, giving an upward momentum to the upper part of the body and also displacing it to the left sufficiently to bring the center of gravity over the feet at the moment of landing.

34. *Back vault* (*Rear vault*). This is the last of the three horizontal vaults. The back is toward the apparatus at the moment of passing it. The approach, placing of the hands and spring from the floor are exactly like those of the "Side vault." But as the legs are raised, say to the left, the trunk remains more nearly vertical, there is a more marked bend to the left at the waist, followed very soon by a 90-degree turn of the whole body to the left, a straightening at the waist and a sharp bend at the hips. As in the "Side vault" the weight is put on the right arm soon after the feet have left the floor, then, just as the legs are passing the apparatus, the left hand is brought behind the back and replaces the right hand in supporting the weight during the descent.

The anatomical mechanism of the various phases of the vault includes: (1) Contraction of the abdominal and lower back muscles of the left side, aided by the abductors of the left and adductors of the right hip joint. (2) The turn of the body begins as a twisting of the hips to left, produced by the oblique abdominal and back muscles. The impulse for the turn of the shoulders is given by the left hand as it releases its hold on the apparatus soon after the feet have left the floor. It involves rotation outward in the right shoulder joint (see below). (3) Flexion at the hips and in the lower back, by the hip joint flexors and abdominal muscles. (4) Rotation outward and hyperextension in the right shoulder joint, and resistance to gravity, tending to produce abduction in this joint, elevation and rotation upward of the scapula and flexion in the right elbow. This requires contraction of the latissimus and teres major; lower pectoralis major, posterior deltoid, infraspinatus and teres minor; pectoralis minor and rhomboids; lower trapezius and the triceps, all on the right side. The turn of the shoulders also necessitates contraction of the oblique abdominal and back muscles of a character reverse to that occurring when the hips are turned at the beginning of the ascent.

During the descent the hips and lower back are straightened, chiefly by gravity, but, as the movement is quick, the hip and back extensors also assist by a momentary contraction. The weight having been transferred to the left arm, gravity and what is left of the initial momentum now produce abduction combined with flexion and slight rotation inward in the left shoulder joint, rotation upward with tendency to elevation and abduction of the left scapula. The left elbow also is apt to bend. The active muscles are those which resist these movements or tendencies, viz., the left latissimus and teres major, lower pectoralis major; pectoralis minor and rhomboids; lower and middle trapezius; and triceps.

35. *The Hand stand* is reached by a movement the first part of which is like "Free Front Rest" as far as the shoulder region is concerned. But in raising the legs and inverting the body to the "Hand stand" there is at first a considerable bend at the hips and more flexion in the elbows than occurs in "Free Front Rest."

When the trunk has passed the horizontal its further elevation and final inversion involve continued flexion and then extension with rotation outward and abduction in the shoulder joint and rotation upward of the scapula, until the limits of these movements are approached. This is equivalent to a forward-upward arm raising and is accomplished by the contraction of the deltoid and supraspinatus, trapezius and serratus, infraspinatus and teres minor, aided, of course, by the momentum developed in the spring from the floor. The rhomboids and levator anguli scapulæ also become active, aiding the upper trapezius in resisting the tendency of gravity to depress the scapula as the vertical, inverted position of the trunk is approached. Just before this is reached the hips, lower back and elbows are straightened by the forcible contraction of their respective extensor muscles.

The final position is usually rather arched, demanding static contraction of the abdominal and pectoral muscles, while the shoulder joint and scapula are kept in their respective positions by continued complete contraction of the muscles which brought them there (see above).  The balance is maintained by constant small adjustments involving interplay between the anterior and posterior muscles, supplemented by alternate quick yieldings and recoveries on the part of the triceps.

The exercise calls for and develops a high degree of coördination, a keen sense of equilibrium and considerable strength. If the tendency to excessive arching in the lower back is resisted, its influence on posture is on the whole favorable.

36.  *The vertical vaults.*  This group comprises the "Squat" and "Straddle" vaults and their combination, the "half Squat half Straddle" vault ("wolf" vault); the "Rear Squat" and "Rear Straddle" vaults; the "Knee" vault and "Front" vault ("Sheep" vault); the "Cross-legged" vault; and the "Jump" vault ("Thief" vault).  As far as the shoulder region is concerned, the mechanism is very nearly the same in all of them, with the exception of the "Jump" vault.

The *Front vault* may serve as illustration, being the simplest in its mechanism, although by no means easy of execution.  It is preceded by a run, culminating in a short, quick jump and then a take-off or spring from both feet.  The arms are drawn back on the jump, then quickly swung forward.  The hands are placed on the apparatus an instant after the spring has been made.

At this moment the shoulder joint is. in 'a position of partial flexion, the scapula somewhat abducted, elevated and rotated upward.  As the arms receive the weight the elbows bend a little; then follow immediately, and practically simultaneously, extension in the elbow and shoulder joints, rotation downward, adduction and depression of the scapula, all together constituting a spring from the hands.  It results from the sudden contraction of the triceps, pectorals, rhomboids, latissimus and teres major. It serves to increase the momentum gained by the spring from the feet and to deflect it in a more upward direction.  On the quickness and vigor of this muscular effort depends also, primarily, the erect, vertical position of the body during the progress of the vault.  This position, however, cannot be attained perfectly, nor can the apparatus be cleared by the feet successfully, without a supplementary forcible contraction of all the longitudinal back muscles and the hip joint extensors, occurring just as the ascent is being completed.  This insures a good fundamental position of the whole body as the apparatus is cleared, chest leading, feet last.  The only discrepancies are a rather excessive hyperextension in the lumbar spine and more or less bend at the knees, both faults being almost impossible to eliminate.

In the *Jump vault* the spring is from one foot, just as in the ordinary straight jump.  The feet then pass the apparatus first, the body is slightly inclined backward, and the hands touch only after the descent has begun. The spring from the hands in this case involves hyperextension in the shoulder joint, almost always associated with elevation and tilting forward of the scapula on its median horizontal axis. The muscular effort is similar to that occurring in the "Front vault," with the action of the pectoralis minor, latissimus and teres major predominating. On account of the marked displacement of the scapula and the forward position of the head so common in this vault, it has a rather unfavorable tendency as regards posture in the upper part of the body.

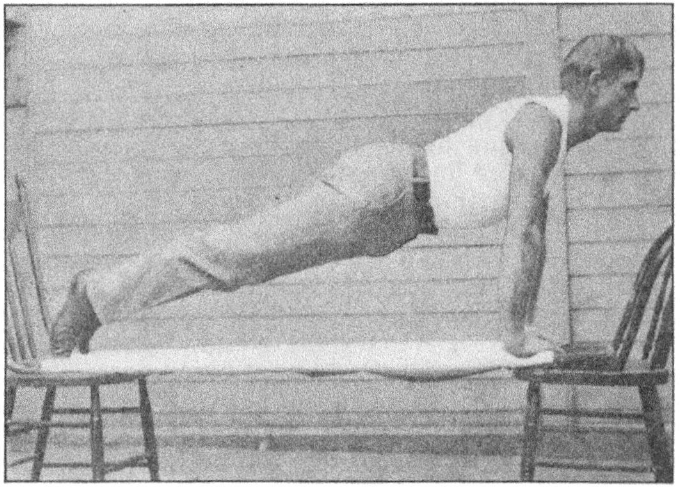

FIGURE 24

PRONE FALLING POSITION (FRONT LEANING REST)

37. *Prone falling position* (Front Leaning Rest). The body weight is here supported in part on the hands, in part on the feet (toes). When the hands are on a considerably higher level than the feet, with the body inclined 45°, the muscular mechanism in the upper part of the body is similar to that of "Front Rest." When the hands and feet are on the same level—as the floor or parallel bars, with the body nearly horizontal—the difference is greater; not so much as regards the particular muscles employed —for they are practically the same—but more in regard to the rôle gravity plays in inducing this muscular interplay, acting, as it does, almost perpendicularly to the whole length axis of the body. The balance element, so prominent and complicating a

factor in "Front Rest," is wholly absent in the "Prone falling position."

It will be assumed· that the position is taken on the floor, with the hands directly under the shoulders—or a few inches nearer the feet—and the fingers turned diagonally toward each other. The shoulder joint is then in a state of partial flexion and rotation inward, gravity tending to produce abduction and extension in this joint and flexion in the elbow. Gravity also tends to adduct the scapula and to displace it bodily in a direction away from the back. At the same time the abdomen and hips tend to "sag" and the knees to bend. This means hyperextension in the lower back accompanied by increased flexion in the upper thoracic spine, diminished flexion in the shoulder joint, elevation and rotation upward of the scapula added to the displacement of this bone already mentioned. The muscles directly concerned in resisting these tendencies are the triceps; the abdominal muscles; the anterior adductor and the flexors of the shoulder joint—the pectoralis major, anterior deltoid, coraco-brachialis and short head of biceps; the abductors, rotators downward and depressors of the scapula—pectoralis minor and rhomboids, serratus magnus and lower trapezius.

The difficulties and common faults of the position, with the muscular action required in overcoming them, may be grouped under two heads: (1) those due to insufficient muscular resistance to gravity; (2) those associated with excessive muscular efforts to resist gravity.

(1) In the first category belongs what might be called the "relaxed" position, in which the weight is simply passively suspended on the muscles. Gravity then has free play and the extreme sagging of the lower trunk and hips with rounding of the upper back and mal-position of the scapula are the results. The proper contraction with moderate shortening of the muscles enumerated above corrects this.

(2) The other type of faulty position occurs as the result of excessive, unbalanced contraction of the abdominal muscles (usually with associated action of the hip joint flexors), the pectorals and the serratus magnus. This leads to a rounding of the whole back, accompanied by flexion at the hips. Or, if the abdominal muscles are managed properly, so that the lower back and hips are kept straight, the pectorals and serratus may still contract excessively, causing an extreme forward displacement of the shoulder girdle, depression of the chest and rounding of upper back. To insure a straight, flat upper back with proper scapular fixation the action of the pectorals and serratus must be balanced by contraction of the lower and middle trapezius, the rhomboids and the upper prolongations of the erector spinæ.

In *Arm bending* from this position, with the elbows moving well sideways, the triceps, pectorals and anterior deltoid are allowed to yield to gravity, while the scapular adductors and the upper back muscles should remain strongly contracted. In this way the movement may be done without disturbing the position of the chest, back and shoulder blades (compare arm bending from "Cross Rest").

38. *Cross Rest* on the parallel bars. The body is in the fundamental position, vertical, supported entirely on the straight arms, one hand on each bar. Gravity tends to flex the elbow, abduct and hyperextend the shoulder joint, elevate the scapula and rotate it upward. The muscles maintaining the position are therefore the triceps; the (flexors and) adductors of the shoulder joint—the pectoralis major (anterior deltoid), latissimus and teres major; the depressors and rotators downward of the scapula —pectoralis minor, rhomboids and (lower) trapezius.

FIGURE 25

ARM BENDING FROM PRONE FALLING POSITION

The proper posture in the upper part of the body is, as usual, dependent on the vigorous contraction of the adductors and depressors of the scapula; rhomboids, trapezius and latissimus. While the amount of work demanded of these muscles is considerable, their action is comparatively simple, being more in line with, and therefore less opposed to, that of the pectorals than is the case in "Front Rest" and the "Prone falling position." There is no difficult balance problem to complicate matters. The lower back and hips are kept straight and rigid by moderate contraction of both anterior and posterior muscles of the lower trunk and hip region.

*Walking forward or backward* on the hands from this position involves the above-mentioned muscular action on one side at a time. Because of the excessive amount of weight supported momentarily on one arm, the working muscles are rarely equal to their task. This leads in the majority of cases to marked disturbance of the posture of the chest, upper back and scapula. It is another case of excessive pectoral action induced by gravity, and of the scapular depressors and adductors working against too great odds and therefore unable to cope with the situation. For this reason the exercise is an undesirable one and should under no circumstances be given to any but strong and well-trained individuals.

39. *Arm bending from Cross Rest.* (The "dip" and push-up.) The muscles active in maintaining the fundamental position in "Cross Rest" yield to gravity. The resulting movement consists of flexion in the elbow, hyper-extension combined with abduction in the shoulder joint, elevation with slight abduction and rotation upward of the scapula, and finally a tilting forward of this bone on its transverse axis in such a manner that its lower angle is moved backward and upward, away from the posterior surface of the thorax. This peculiar displacement is associated with a forward position of the point of the shoulder, rounding of the upper back and depression of the chest. The whole mal-position is due to some extent to the powerful action of the pectorals in their efforts to resist the scapular elevation produced by gravity. A similar displacement is apt to occur in any exercise involving support of a large part of the weight on the arms, such as "Front Rest," "Prone falling position," "Cross Rest." But in all these it may be prevented and the scapula kept in proper apposition to the back by a sufficiently vigorous contraction of the scapular adduc-

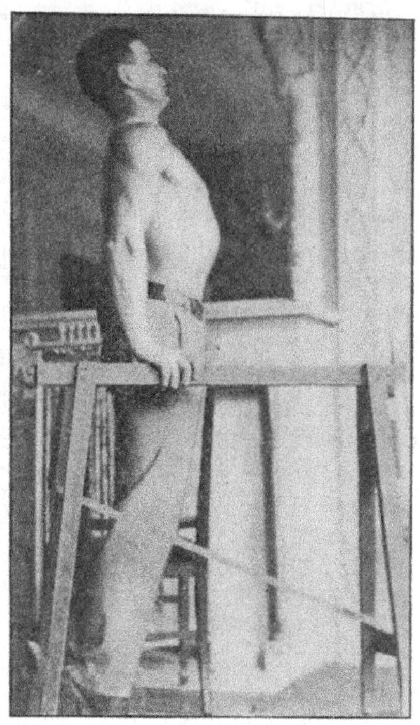

FIGURE 26

CROSS REST

tors and posterior depressors. In this exercise—the "dip"—the abnormal position of the shoulder girdle and upper trunk is not only of the most pronounced character, but *cannot be prevented,* no matter how strong or well-trained the individual. The explanation is simple enough. When the elbow bends the humerus moves almost directly backward, i.e., there occurs at first hyper-extension in the shoulder joint. The amount of this permitted in the joint is very small, however (from 5° to 10°). When this is checked by the complete stretching of the anterior part of the capsular ligament of the shoulder joint, the two bones—humerus and scapula—are virtually one. Gravity, acting with good leverage through the humerus, then *pries* the scapula into the abnormal position described above. The only structures that can hold the bone down are the

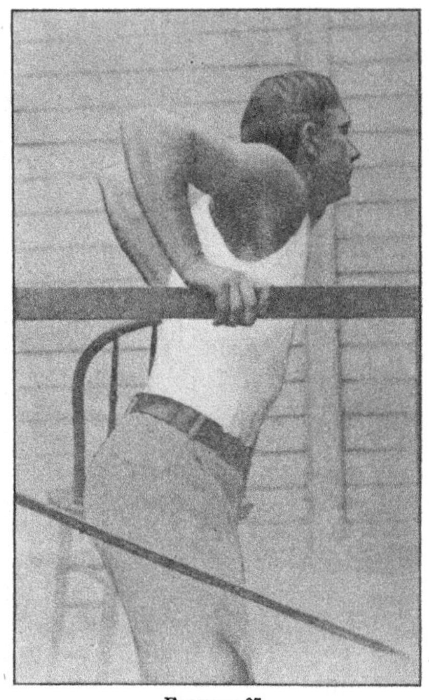

FIGURE 27

ARM BENDING FROM CROSS REST

(serratus) trapezius and rhomboid muscles, the fasciæ and the skin. These stretch as far as possible; then, if the movement proceeds further, the upper trunk must follow the humerus in its backward-upward sweep. This is what actually happens and accounts for the extreme rounding of the upper thoracic spine and depression of the chest so characteristic in this exercise.

The return movement—the "push-up"—is accomplished by the contraction of the triceps, pectorals and rhomboids, aided by the short head of biceps, coraco-brachialis and anterior deltoid. As was pointed out in the analysis of the faulty type of "Front Rest" the extreme contraction of the pectorals against great resistance tends to bring the muscles of each side into line with each other, unless their action is balanced by vigorous contraction of their antagonists posteriorly. In this case such neutralizing action is rarely if ever sufficient, so that, while it is possible to return to the correct position of "Cross Rest," the usual thing is that the mal-position of scapula, back and chest remains more or less as the arms are straightened and the body lifted. The final return position very often resembles the faulty "Front Rest."

Considering the mechanical peculiarities of this movement, making a good posture in the upper part of the body practically impossible during the greater part of both the descent and the ascent; inducing, as it does, excessive, unbalanced action of the pectorals with almost complete shortening throughout; and bearing in mind the fundamental principle that the body tends to retain permanently the postures it assumes when in action, the vicious tendency of this exercise from a postural standpoint should be perfectly obvious. Yet it is one of the most widely known and practiced exercises in the gymnasium. It is usually the first thing that a new "member" attempts. It seems to appeal to young men and boys, because, for one thing, it involves severe muscular work of a rather uncomfortable kind, and the ability to repeat the exercise many times is therefore presumably an index of his strength and "hardness." This idea is no doubt fostered by the fact that the exercise is, unfortunately, one of the routine strength tests used in colleges and many other institutions. Again, the extreme contraction and tension of the pectorals give rise to sensations which are somewhat similar to those associated with chest expansion, and this leads the lay performer to think that he is doing something which is "very good for chest development." In this thought he is not infrequently encouraged by the person in charge. But, fortunately, the number of teachers who are willing to endorse exercises of this type is rapidly diminishing.

While the simple type on the parallel bars has been selected for purposes of analysis, there are many exercises (more properly "stunts" or "tricks") on the parallel bars, horizontal bar and rings, in which the mechanism is identical. The so-called "swinging dip," by many supposed to be less objectionable than the "still dip," differs in no essential respect from the latter, as far as the shoulder region is concerned. The same is true of the pushing down of the traveling or wall parallels, although this is milder because the resistance is not so great. What has been said about the "dip" is true more or less of any movement in which the arm swings excessively backward in the sagittal plane, whether moved by the individual's own muscular efforts, by his weight, or by external forces.

The training of the chest muscles and triceps, which is the chief end sought by those who practice such exercises in good faith, may be accomplished as effectively in other ways, e.g., by exercises with the chest weights, back to the weights; by work on suspension apparatus with the hands far apart; and by arm bending from the "Prone falling position" with the elbows moving well sideways. In all these it is at least possible to keep the upper trunk erect, the back flat and the chest expanded, and so to favor, rather than impair, a permanent good posture by the very difficulties successfully overcome.

### D. SWIMMING, ROWING, PADDLING, THROWING.

40. *The arm movement in breast stroke swimming* may be conveniently divided into three parts. (1) Placing the hands in front of the chest. This involves, besides flexion at the elbow and wrist, a slight flexion with a little abduction in the shoulder joint, accompanied, as usual, with some rotation upward of the scapula. (2) The thrusting forward of the hands. This would be equivalent to an arm stretching forward-upward, if the body were in the upright position. Anatomically it means extension in the elbow and wrist joints, flexion in the shoulder joint and considerable rotation upward with abduction of the scapula. The active muscles are, therefore, the triceps; the upper pectoralis major, anterior (and central) deltoid, short (and long) head of biceps and coraco-brachialis; the trapezius and serratus magnus. (3) The stroke proper, which would correspond to a backward-downward sweep of the arms, with the palms turned downward and backward, if the body were in the upright position; in other words, extension with at first abduction, then adduction, as well as rotation inward in the shoulder joint; rotation downward with adduction of the scapula; and pronation in the forearm. The motor muscles are the posterior and central deltoid, the latissimus and teres major, the lower pectoralis major and subscapularis; the pectoralis minor and rhomboids; the central and lower trapezius. The longitudinal back and posterior neck muscles maintain a vigorous contraction throughout. As will readily be seen, the mechanism is such as to compel a correct posture of the head, chest, shoulders and back, and the exercise is generally recognized as a valuable one for purposes of postural improvement.

41. *Rowing.* The straight backed type will be assumed, with the body swinging behind as well as in front of the vertical (about 30° to 40° each way; fixed seat).

When the oars catch, the body is bent sharply at the hips, the lower back is straight or flexed (in individuals whose lumbar spines are capable of that), the elbow is extended, the shoulder joint flexed, the scapula partially abducted, rotated upward and elevated. The stroke begins with extension in the hip and lumbar spine. This continues throughout and is supplemented toward the end by flexion in the elbow; extension combined at first with abduction followed by adduction in the shoulder joint, as well as some rotation outward in this joint; adduction with rotation downward of the scapula. The active muscles are the erector spinæ and hip joint extensors, the biceps and brachialis anticus, the central and posterior deltoid and the supraspinatus, the infraspinatus and teres minor, the latissimus and teres major, the rhomboids and trapezius (lower and central portions). Conscious effort is necessary to keep the head back, the upper back straight and the shoulders low. This requires partial relaxation of the anterior, and contraction of the posterior neck muscles, as well as additional work on the part of the scapular depressors (principally the lower trapezius and the latissimus). The recovery is accomplished by the contraction of the abdominal muscles and hip joint flexors until the vertical position of the trunk has been passed. After that, gravity is the chief motor force in causing further bend at the hips, and in the lower back. At the same time the arms are thrust forward by extension in the elbow, flexion, with at first abduction, then adduction and gradual rotation inward in the shoulder joint, abduction and rotation upward of the scapula. (The feathering of the oar is the result of hyperextension in the wrist joint.) These movements are produced by the triceps; the upper pectoralis major, anterior deltoid, coraco-brachialis and short head of the biceps; the serratus magnus and trapezius. While the hip joint extensors and lower erector spinæ relax during the first part of the recovery, they begin to contract "eccentrically"—resisting gravity—soon after the vertical has been passed. The posterior neck muscles and upper erector spinæ have to be in action all the time, if the head and upper back are to be kept erect. The same is true of the scapular adductors. Rowing of this type is favorable to good posture, besides being an excellent general exercise.

42. *Paddling.* Assume that the left hand is high, right hand low. The position at the beginning of the stroke has been reached by a twisting of the trunk to left and a slight bend to right at the waist; by flexion combined with a little abduction in both shoulder joints, more in the left than in the right; by abduction with rotation upward of both scapulæ, the right more than the left. The left scapula is also elevated somewhat and there is usually a partial flexion in the left elbow joint.

The stroke consists of a twist to the right of the trunk with a straightening and even slight bend to the left at the waist; then on the right side, extension combined with increased abduction and some rotation inward in the shoulder joint; moderate adduction and rotation downward of the scapula; pronation in the forearm and usually some flexion in the elbow. On the left side there occur: extension in the elbow; extension with adduction in the shoulder joint; abduction of the scapula. As the stroke progresses the trunk is also raised a little by slight extension in the hip joints. The motor muscles are therefore the oblique abdominal and back muscles and the extensors of the hip joint and back. On the right side: the latissimus, teres major, posterior and central deltoid (and supraspinatus), lower pectoralis major, rhomboids and trapezius, triceps (at first). On the left side: the triceps, lower pectoralis major, pectoralis minor, serratus magnus, latissimus and teres major.

43. *Throwing.* The ordinary overhand type will be assumed. The arm is raised, at first a little forward, then sideways-upward and backward, and the hand brought behind and above the shoulder, preparatory to the delivery, by flexion in the elbow, flexion, abduction and rotation outward in the shoulder joint, and adduction of the scapula. At the same time, the trunk is twisted to the right, the weight is shifted to the right foot, and the advance of the left foot is begun. The motor muscles for this part of the movement are the biceps, etc., the deltoid, infraspinatus and teres minor; the trapezius and rhomboids, the oblique abdominal and back muscles which rotate the trunk to the right.

The throw proper, or delivery, consists in the first place of a twisting of the trunk to the left with transfer of the weight to the advancing left foot. At the same time the segments of the upper extremity execute a series of movements which may be described as abduction with rotation upward of the scapula, a forward movement of the humerus, while remaining horizontal (bringing the shoulder joint to a position of flexion from a position of abduction with rotation outward). Then follow extension in the elbow, and straightening of the wrist (previously hyperextended). The muscles responsible for this part of the movement are: the oblique abdominal and back muscles which rotate the trunk to the left (as well as the extensors of the right hip and knee joints); the serratus magnus and pectoralis minor; the pectoralis major, subscapularis and anterior deltoid; the triceps (and the flexors of the wrist joint).

The amount of momentum developed depends largely on the proper sequence and increasing speed of the movements of the various segments, from the center to the periphery. This includes keeping the elbow in front of the hand until the last moment.

## B.  LOWER TRUNK AND HIP REGION.

The Need and Value of Motor Training in This Region.

In analyzing the mechanism of movements involving the shoulder and upper trunk region, attention was frequently called to the close association of the joints and muscles of the arm, shoulder girdle and upper spine.  Unless conscious effort is made to avoid it, any movement of one of these parts is apt to be distributed to the other two, thereby changing their relative positions. The definitions of most of the movements described were such as to require inhibition, or breaking up, of some of those natural associations on the one hand, and on the other to cultivate new and sometimes rather difficult associations.  The purpose of such definitions is to induce under all conditions well coördinated action of the muscles responsible for good posture of head, neck, shoulders, upper back and chest; to maintain and to increase mobility of the joints in directions where mobility gradually tends to diminish; and to train the power of localization of movement with a view gradually to increase the ability to localize muscular contraction.  This ultimately makes for efficiency and economy of effort.  Repeated successful efforts of this kind, under increasing difficulties, give the individual the sense of good posture, teach him how to assume it, and, we hope, give him the ambition as well as the ability to form better postural and motor habits.  In the growing individual we may reasonably expect that by persistent practice of gymnastic exercises of this kind (with a good, erect posture maintained throughout) the structural relations, as well as the motor habits, will be most favorably influ- . enced.  It is a case of "bending the twig" in the direction we wish it to grow.

In the lower trunk and hip region, the relations as regards movements and positions of the various parts—spine, pelvis and lower extremity—are analogous to those existing in the upper trunk and shoulder region.  It is very difficult, if not impossible, to make extensive or powerful movements of one without involving the others.  Postural relations are equally interdependent. Here, even more than in the upper trunk and shoulder, gravity plays an important rôle, as the region is especially adapted for weight-bearing.  Any considerable deviation from the straight line, or any inequality or asymmetry in one place may always be expected to involve compensatory adjustment above or below. For example, if the right leg is longer than the left, the right hip will be higher or project more than the left, and the lower spine will be curved with the convexity to the left. Similarly, if the leg is raised quickly and forcibly to one side, the pelvis will be tilted and the lumbar spine convex to the opposite side. Again, such an exercise as leg raising backward is entirely a displacement of the pelvis involving movement of complex character in the opposite hip joint and the lumbar spine. In short, any extensive movement of the femur is accompanied by changes in the position of the pelvis, brought about chiefly by movement in the lumbar spine. This is partly due to the relatively limited range of motion in the hip joint (as compared with the shoulder joint), partly, as in the shoulder region, to the close functional association of the muscles. Finally, even slight movements in one or both hip joints in the upright position involve changes of posture in the pelvis and lumbar spine on account of the redistribution of the weight which is a necessary concomitant in such movements.

The need for varied and systematic training of the large and powerful neuromuscular mechanisms of this region is perhaps not as fully recognized as in the case of the upper trunk and shoulder region. The relatively limited scope and variety of movements in the lower part of the body, the usually vague and undefined character of their combinations and the naturally close association of many of the muscle groups might suggest on the one hand that this is not a very fertile field for the cultivation of fine distinctions and delicate adjustment of movement; on the other, that if any results in these directions are attainable, they may not represent enough value to be worth striving for. But a little observation and analysis will show that the motor adjustments in this region, while not as extensive and varied as in the shoulder region, owing to the greater prominence of the supporting function, are nevertheless more numerous and complex than at first might appear. Many of them are capable of division into their component elements, which may be trained separately or rearranged in new combinations, thereby improving the power of localization, eliminating unnecessary or undesirable features, increasing variety and accuracy of adjustment and so enlarging the individual's subjective control and his adaptability to his environment.

The perfect automatism of a great many coördinations having to do with locomotion and the upright position and acquired so long ago that we are unaware of their existence or have dismissed them from our minds as of no further interest, is partly responsible for the tendency to neglect the finer motor training in this region. Here, even more than is the case in the upper part of the body, we are apt to let things be "as the Lord made them." Because of the deeply grooved motor and postural habits, because of the fundamental character of many associated movements, we are loth to attempt to modify or break up these deeply rooted associations. The difficulties encountered are undoubtedly great and the results not always as encouraging as we should like. But such considerations should not deter us from trying to improve and diversify motor control in this region by selecting, defining and teaching gymnastic exercises that demand the utmost efforts on the part of our pupils to assume and retain under all conditions the best posture of which they are capable; to move with speed and precision, or with deliberation and steadiness; to appreciate small differences of plane, direction, rhythm, momentum, etc. The ability to localize movement and even to some extent muscular contraction in this region is one of the factors which determine the gait. Proper weight distribution is another. The sense of balance and rhythm is equally important in this respect. All of these elements influence posture, not only in the lower part of the body, but in the upper as well. All contribute largely to the general bearing of the individual, to the degree of grace and efficiency of his movements. All may be cultivated by carefully defined and properly executed gymnastic exercises. If the teaching and guidance are what they should be, and if the pupils can be induced to put forth the requisite effort between, as well as during, the lessons, the right kind of motor ideals, concepts and habits can in this way be most effectively conveyed and inculcated.

From the physiological standpoint vigorous movements of the lower trunk and extremity rank first in importance. Strong contractions of the abdominal and lower trunk muscles and of the large groups of hip and thigh muscles profoundly influence the functions of all the great vital organs. In this respect, as well as regards the training of good posture and motor control, definite, clean-cut, localized movements are probably more effective than movements of the opposite character, if for no other reason than that they demand more work in a given time. However, the advantage of this style of work is here less obvious. In the beginning, before a sufficient amount of coördination has been acquired, it is admittedly less effective, as time has to be spent in drilling certain fundamental details which require a relatively small amount of muscular action, or at any rate break up the continuity of the work.

### Anatomical Review.

Before taking up the discussion of the mechanism of gymnastic movements, a résumé of the principal anatomical facts, which form a basis for such discussion, will be of advantage.

I. JOINTS.

1. *The lumbar spine.* On account of the relative thickness of the intervertebral disks and the comparative laxness of the capsular and other ligaments, flexion, extension and lateral bendings are freer here than in any other part of the spine. The normal position of the region is one of hyperextension, that is, concave posteriorly. This may be carried considerably further. The opposite movement, starting from extreme hyperextension, to and a little beyond the straight line, leading to a slight reversal of the normal curve (in the average young person at least), must all be included in the term flexion, as there is no term which describes the return from the position of hyperextension. Sometimes the term straightening will be used to express this. In flexion, extension and hyperextension, as well as in lateral bendings, the two or three lowest thoracic vertebræ move as the lumbar, but less extensively. They may therefore be considered as belonging to the lumbar region in these respects.

Rotation—a twisting of the column on an axis passing through the bodies of the vertebræ—is very limited, owing to the plane of the surfaces by which the articular processes meet. These surfaces are vertical and face more or less inward and outward, so that true rotation, involving a gliding of these surfaces on each other, is effectively prevented by the locking of the articular processes. There is, however, a slight amount of movement corresponding to rotation, made possible by the fact that the articular surfaces do not approximate each other very closely. This looseness of fit, and the leeway thus allowed, in conjunction with successive alternation of flexion, lateral movement and extension between contiguous vertebræ, result in a kind of spiral movement which to a limited extent (amounting to perhaps from 5° to 15°) takes the place of true rotation.

2. *The sacro-iliac joint.* The sacrum is wedge-shaped both from above downward and from before backward. The planes of its articular surfaces and those of the ilia even in the normal position are oblique, converging backward and upward, so that the upper end of the sacrum, receiving the weight of the whole trunk, tends to be displaced forward and downward, the lower end backward and upward. The sacro-iliac ligaments, anterior and posterior, and especially the latter, limit this tilting of the sacrum and prevent it from slipping away from between the ilia. The strong, short fibres of the posterior ligaments are the chief agents in transmitting the weight of the trunk to the ilia, especially when the pelvis is carried in a position of greater than normal obliquity. Under the opposite conditions, that is, when the plane of the pelvis is nearer the horizontal than under.

normal conditions, the sacrum is tilted in such a way as to approach the vertical. Its upper end is then wedged in between the ilia, spreading them apart. In this case a part of the weight is transmitted directly from one bone to the other, causing excessive pressure of the joint surfaces on each other. Both extremes of posture predispose to pathological conditions in the joints (Goldthwaite).

These movements of the sacrum on a horizontal axis always accompany movements in the lumbar spine and hip joint. While they are very limited in extent, the fact that they occur at all under normal conditions, even in adult males, is of interest from a gymnastic standpoint chiefly on account of the influence of posture on the maintenance or restoration of healthy conditions in the joints, as shown by Goldthwaite's recent investigation of this subject.*

3. *The hip joint.* The deep acetabular cavity and the tight-fitting capsular and ilio-femoral ligaments, while making for strength and security, also reduce to some extent the mobility of the joint. Being a ball and socket joint, all kinds of movement are nevertheless permitted and are fairly free. Extension, however, does not go further than to bring the femur into line with the trunk. Hyperextension, that is, a backward movement of the femur on the pelvis, is prevented by the ilio-femoral ligament, which completely locks the two bones in the position of extension.

Like the shoulder joint the hip joint is surrounded on all sides by muscles or tendons. These serve as accessory, elastic ligaments, checking movements before the proper ligaments have become stretched, thus relieving them from too sudden and violent tension. At the same time this intimate muscular connection between the two bones leads to a participation of the pelvis in the movements of the femur long before the limits of motion in the hip joint have been reached. The muscles, with the ilio-femoral ligament, also steady the pelvis on the femur in the upright position, and especially in movements and transitory or sustained positions on one leg.

II.   MUSCLES.

1. *The flexors of the lumbar and lower thoracic spine* are the straight and oblique abdominal muscles. Being attached to the brim of the pelvis and the lower circumference of the thorax, they will draw these two points together. This can only be done by flexion in the lower spine, that is, by a straightening and reversal of the natural anteriorly convex curve in this region.

---

*A Consideration of the Pelvic Articulations from an Anatomical, Pathological and Clinical Standpoint. J. E. Goldthwaite and R. B. Osgood, *Boston Medical and Surgical Journal*, CLII., 21 and 22, pp. 593-634.

This movement may be called flexion of the trunk on the pelvis, or of the pelvis on the trunk, according to which is the more fixed part.

If flexion in the lower spine is prevented by contraction of the extensors, shortening of the abdominal muscles will cause retraction of the abdomen, with or without depression of the chest according to the amount of resistance offered by the muscles of inspiration.

*The extensors of the lower spine* are the erector spinæ and its primary divisions, the lower fibres of the spinalis and semi-spinalis dorsi, the lower multifidus spinæ and the lumbar inter-spinales. All of these will be referred to as the erector spinæ group or as the lower erector spinæ.

*The muscles which are active in lateral bendings of the spine* are the abdominal muscles, the erector spinæ (including the intertransversales), the quadratus lumborum, the serratus posticus inferior and under some conditions the latissimus dorsi, all on one side. Whether the muscles on the side toward which the movement takes place or those on the opposite side are active depends on the relation of gravity or external forces to the movement.

*The rotators of the spine* to the left are: The left serratus posticus inferior, the left erector spinæ and its divisions, the left internal oblique abdominal muscle; the right serratus posticus superior, the right semi-spinalis dorsi, the right multifidus spinæ, the right rotatores spinæ, the right levatores costarum, the right external oblique abdominal muscle.

2. *The hip joint muscles:*

*Flexors:* Psoas and iliacus; sartorius; rectus femoris; pectineus; adductor longus, adductor brevis; pyriformis.

*Extensors:* Gluteus maximus, gluteus medius (posterior portion); the so-called hamstring muscles—biceps (flexor cruris), semitendinosus, semimembranosus.

*Abductors:* Gluteus maximus; gluteus medius; gluteus minimus; tensor fasciæ latæ (also the deep rotators, except the obturator externus, in the sitting position).

*Adductors:* Adductor magnus; adductor longus; adductor brevis; pectineus; gracilis.

*Rotators inward:* Tensor fasciæ latæ; gluteus medius (anterior part); gluteus minimus (anterior part).

*Rotators outward:* Gluteus maximus; gluteus medius (posterior); psoas and iliacus; sartorius, pectineus; the three adductors; the deep rotators—pyriformis, obturator internus, gemelli, obturator externus, quadratus femoris.

It will be seen from the above that many of the muscles

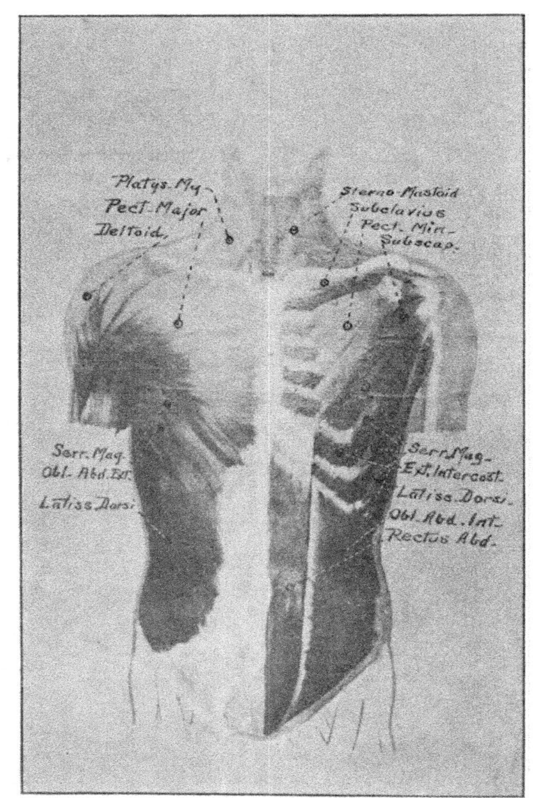

Platys. My.
Pect. Major
Deltoid.
Sterno-Mastoid
Subclavius
Pect. Min.
Subscap.
Serr. Mag.
Obl. Abd. Ext.
Latiss. Dorsi
Serr. Mag.
Ext. Intercost.
Latiss. Dorsi
Obl. Abd. Int.
Rectus Abd.


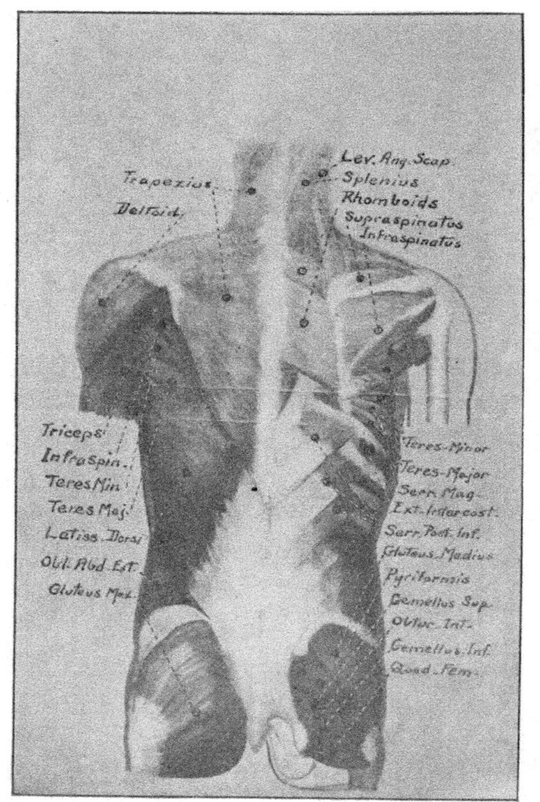

Trapezius
Deltoid.
Lev. Ang. Scap.
Splenius
Rhomboids
Supraspinatus
Infraspinatus
Triceps
Infraspin.
Teres Min.
Teres Maj.
Latiss. Dorsi
Obl. Abd. Ext.
Gluteus Max.
Teres-Minor
Teres-Major
Serr. Mag.
Ext. Intercost.
Serr. Post. Inf.
Gluteus Medius
Pyriformis
Gemellus Sup.
Obtur. Int.
Gemellus Inf.
Quad. Fem.

enumerated act in more than one capacity, in that respect resembling the varied actions of many or most of the muscles in the shoulder region. The reasons are the same, viz.: (1) the extensive lines of attachment of some of the muscles, as the glutei, by which different portions of the same muscle act from opposite directions and under different mechanical conditions, such as leverage, obliquity of pull, etc.; (2) the proximity of many muscles to the joint, and their oblique direction with reference to two or more axes of motion, as, for example, the tensor fasciæ latæ, the sartorius, the gluteus maximus and the deep rotators. They are thereby able to contribute to several kinds of movement or to act differently in different positions of the joint.

The action of the hip joint muscles is further complicated, in certain movements, by the fact that some of them are attached directly or indirectly (through the fascia lata) to the lower leg and thus produce movement or influence positions in the knee joint. Notable examples of this are the rectus femoris, the sartorius and gracilis, and the hamstring muscles. Owing to this the mechanism of many movements in the hip joint varies as regards degree, kind and complexity of muscular action, according to accompanying movements, or inhibition of movements, in the knee joint.

## Gymnastic Movements and Positions.

### A.  DIFFERENT TYPES OF STANDING POSITION.

1. The distribution of weight and its relation to posture in the lower spine, the hip and knee joints vary considerably in different types of habitual, easy standing position. In the best of these the thoracic curve is moderate, long and even, the lumbar curve low and not too sharp. The weight line passes in front of, but fairly close to the thoracic spine; through the bodies of the upper lumbar vertebræ, behind the lower; slightly behind the hip joint; and through, or a little in front of, the center of the knee joint.

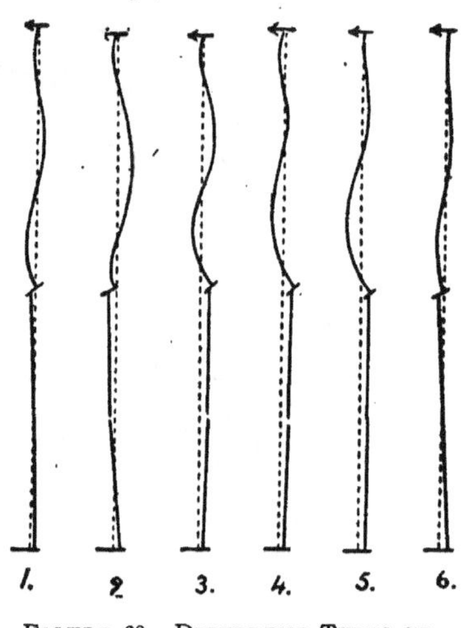



FIGURE 30.  DIFFERENT TYPES OF STANDING POSITION

When the tone of the upper back and abdominal muscles is good, excessive tension on the spinal ligaments and compression of the anterior or posterior edges of the intervertebral disks do not occur, and the spine is balanced and kept in an easy, erect position without much conscious muscular effort.

The slight forward position of the hips with normal pelvic obliquity (the plane of the true pelvis about 60° from the vertical), insures extension in the hip joint. The weight line falling behind the center of this joint, gravity tends to produce hyperextension, but this is prevented by the ilio-femoral ligament, which is put on the stretch when the femur is in line with the trunk. Gravity, in connection with this ligament, thus relieves the extensor muscles from much responsibility in keeping the pelvis steady on the femur and the hip joint in extension.

In the knee joint similar mechanical conditions insure the extended position without much muscular effort. But here the weight line rarely falls far enough in front of the joint to lock it completely, and a very slight shifting of the weight backward makes it fall behind the center of the joint, so that a slight contraction of the quadriceps is often necessary.

2. Of the undesirable variations from the easy standing position described in the preceding paragraph two main types are fairly common. In one of these the hips are carried excessively forward, the lumbar curve is low, not very marked, sometimes almost obliterated; while the thoracic is pronounced and long, often encroaching on the upper lumbar region. The extreme forward position of the hips leads to decreased pelvic obliquity, the plane of the pelvis approaching too nearly the horizontal and the sacrum too nearly the vertical, wedged in between and spreading the ilia. The weight line falls considerably behind the hip joint and also slightly behind the knee joint. This leads to absolute extension in the hip joint with strong tension on the ilio-femoral ligament and allows complete relaxation of the extensor muscles of this joint. The knee joint is often in a state of partial flexion and is kept from further flexion only by a moderate contraction of the quadriceps muscle. This type of relaxed standing position is usually associated with poor general muscular tone and development, the atrophied condition of the gluteal region being particularly striking.

3. In the other type the hips are carried too far back, the lumbar curve is pronounced, long or high, often including the two or three lowest thoracic vertebræ. The thoracic curve is also apt to be excessive, but short and high. The weight line falls well

in front of the thoracic, considerably behind the lumbar spine, and either through or more or less in front of the hip as well as the knee joint. Individuals of this "hollow-back" type are not infrequently strong and heavily muscled, but the upper back and particularly the abdominal muscles are of relatively low tone and habitually relaxed. Gravity acting with good leverage owing to the already excessive curves exerts a strong passive tension on these muscles as well as on the spinal ligaments (pressure on the edges of the disks), and so tends to increase the curves still further. The posterior position of the hips is associated with too great pelvic obliquity, and this in turn means excessive tipping forward of (the upper end of) the sacrum, approximation of the ilia, spreading of the ischia, and too great tension on the sacro-iliac ligaments. The weight line falling in front of the hip joint, gravity constantly tends to increase the partial flexion in this joint, which is another feature associated with too great pelvic obliquity. This necessitates constant moderate contraction of the hip joint extensors. The knee joint is kept locked in the extended position by gravity.

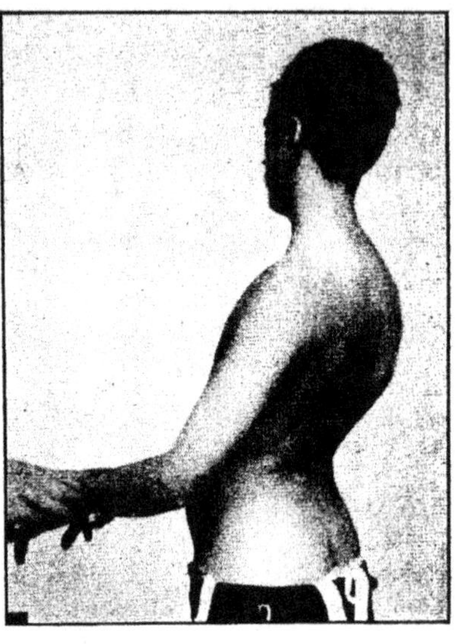

FIG. 31. "HOLLOW BACK" POSITION

4. A third, less common type, resembles the preceding in the excessive, elongated curve of the lumbar region (including the lower thoracic vertebræ), in the increased pelvic obliquity and in the flexed position of the hip joint. It differs from it in the conformation and posture of the upper part of the body, being usually associated with well-shaped chest and shoulders, fairly straight and flat upper back. The muscular tone is good generally, and especially in the back. The abdomen, however, is apt to be somewhat relaxed, but less so than in the preceding type.

5. *Faulty posture in the lower trunk and hip region induced by gymnastic exercises.* Closely resembling the last described variety of relaxed or semi-relaxed posi-

tion, as regards the lower part of the body, is the position with exaggerated and usually high lumbar curve which occurs as a by-product of misdirected or poorly localized efforts to straighten the upper back and to improve the posture of head, chest and shoulders.

All gymnastic standing positions, whether correct or incorrect, differ from all varieties of easy standing position in that conscious, vigorous contraction of the upper back muscles is demanded in order to obtain a good, erect posture in the upper part of the body. The latter may or may not be accomplished, but. in any case the effort nearly always leads to increased lumbar hyperextension and pelvic obliquity. The reasons for this are as follows: Strong contraction of the erector spinæ group cannot, without special training or skill, be confined to the higher levels, the different portions of this group acting as one muscle. This muscular mass is thickest and most compactly arranged in the lower back. Here, running along the naturally concave lumbar spine it works under more favorable mechanical conditions than higher up, where it covers the convex thoracic spine and posterior chest wall. The lumbar spine has much greater freedom of movement, especially in a backward direction, and so offers less resistance, than the thoracic region, encumbered as this is with the relatively rigid and heavy chest. Finally, gravity from the outset favors increased hyperextension in the lower back, while it opposes extension in the thoracic region, at least until the upper trunk has been tilted backward considerably (by hyperextension in the lumbar spine).

The induced lordosis resulting from the general contraction of the whole erector spinæ group in attempts to stand up straight is even more pronounced in many gymnastic exercises involving strong contraction of the posterior scapular muscles and particularly of the latissimus dorsi. These superficial back muscles are closely associated with the erector spinæ group, maximal contraction of one set usually inducing action of the other. The latissimus also acts directly on the lower spine, pulling it forward, as well as indirectly through its pull on the three lowest ribs. Then there are many gymnastic exercises in which powerful contraction of the lower erector spinæ is necessary for successful performance, as, for example, in leg raising backward, prone lying position, and many vaults. There are also some useful exercises in which marked hyperextension due to gravity or to the pull of the psoas and ilicus muscles is an almost unavoidable feature. Examples of this are the prone hanging and the prone falling position, opposite (foot grasp) sitting backward leaning of trunk, the hand stand. All gymnastic exercises tending to produce this abnormal posture in the lower back may be justly criticised on this account and can only be defended on grounds of general or special value in other directions, or by defining and teaching them in such a way that this fault will be largely or wholly eliminated. -In many cases this can be done by patience and persistence in the teaching and by judicious progression. (The muscular action necessary to prevent or correct this faulty posture will be discussed under the fundamental gymnastic standing position.)

Aside from æsthetic considerations, excessive "hollow" in the lower back, whether habitual or induced by conscious muscular contraction, is undesirable for many reasons. The associated abnormal position of the pelvis and its joints has already been mentioned. Discomfort, painful fatigue—popularly referred to as weakness—in the lower back, resulting from long standing in this position, is very common. There is greater liability to injury —sprains of the spinal and sacro-iliac joints—in falls or missteps, partly because the weight acts with greater leverage and on ligaments already stretched; partly and chiefly because in the greatly relaxed condition of the abdominal muscles so commonly associated with lordosis, these muscles fail to give that support to the spinal column and that elastic resistance to sudden excessive hyperextension which would save the joints and ligaments from too great strain. Finally, the marked forward convexity in the lower back and the relaxed abdominal wall allow the abdominal organs, suspended in their mesenteric sling from the upper lumbar spine, to sag unduly forward-downward and deprive them of their proper support, conditions which are inimical to their healthy functioning.

In view of the actual and potential disadvantages of exaggerated curve in the lower back, and because so many gymnastic exercises can be done in a way to produce or aggravate this condition, it should be one of the legitimate objects of gymnastic work and the duty of those who teach it to furnish definite and systematic training of a kind calculated to make this fault less accentuated when it already exists, and to prevent, as far as possible, its occurrence as a by-product of gymnastic movements and positions. In the selection, definition, progression and teaching of the exercises this element should always be reckoned with, and no performance accepted as satisfactory in which the posture in the lower part of the body is markedly defective.

While the muscular tone and control necessary for the prevention and correction of excessive lumbar hyperextension and pelvic obliquity may to some extent be acquired by gymnastic class exercises, it will always be found helpful and sometimes necessary, especially in the beginning, to supplement the general instruction with individual suggestion and help. Actually placing the pupil in the forced correct position by manipulation may be the only way to give him a clear idea of it, to make him acquainted with the bodily sensations which accompany the change in weight distribution and the muscular efforts required to retain it. The memory of these will then serve as a guide in repeated efforts on his part to assume and maintain the correct posture under varying conditions, gymnastic or otherwise.

6. *The gymnastic fundamental standing position.* The definition and mechanism of the fundamental position in the upper trunk and shoulder region has been given in an earlier chapter (page 21). In the lower part of the body conscious effort should be made to straighten the lumbar spine, or at any rate to prevent increased hyperextension; to reduce pelvic obliquity, and to keep the hip joint in complete extension. The postural relations of the spine, pelvis and lower extremity should at least be made to equal those obtaining in the best type of easy standing position, as regards proximity of the different parts to the weight line. In any case the alignment of upper and lower spine, pelvis and leg should be as absolute, and the undulations in front and behind the weight line as limited as individual peculiarities will allow. This demands a strong contraction of the abdominal muscles at all times, and, in the beginning, also of the glutei and hamstring muscles. The effect of the action of both groups is to reduce the obliquity of the pelvis, i.e., to tilt it into a more horizontal position. The abdominal muscles pull its anterior margin upward and forward, the glutei and hamstring muscles pull its posterior portion downward. The resulting movement involves extension in the hip joint, and straightening of the lumbar spine. By this muscular effort the pelvis is also displaced forward sufficiently to bring the hip joint in front of the weight line. Gravity then aids in keeping this joint in the extended position by acting against and stretching the ilio-femoral ligament situated in front of the joint. The whole movement may be termed flexion of the pelvis on the trunk, the

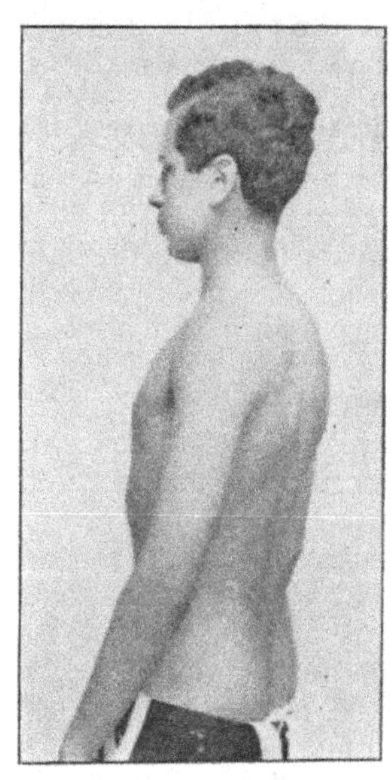

FIGURE 32
CORRECTED "HOLLOW BACK" POSITION

hip joint extension being incidental, due to the relative fixation of the lower end of the femur in the standing position. By this movement of the pelvis, produced by concerted action of the abdominal muscles, the hip joint extensors and gravity, the excessive action of the lower erector spinæ, instinctively associated with all efforts to straighten the upper back, is balanced and its effects neutralized: marked hyperextension in the lumbar spine is prevented, the natural curve may even be almost obliterated, the pelvis is kept from being displaced backward and its obliquity is reduced.

Simple as this muscular effort and redistribution of weight appear, they are rather difficult to learn and to teach. What usually happens at first is that, as soon as the lower back and pelvis are brought into the desired position, there is a "slump" in the upper part of the body, due to a relaxation of all the back muscles. It is another example of the difficulty of dissociating the action of the different parts of complex neuromuscular mechanisms, habitually working together as units, of inhibiting the action of some parts, while others remain in strong contraction, of adjusting and harmonizing the action of the latter to the partly antagonistic action of other forces in order to obtain new combinations of movements or position. The opposing forces in this case are on one hand the whole erector spinæ group and the posterior scapular muscles working together to produce extension (and hyperextension) of the trunk on the pelvis in a general way, and incidentally leading to one kind of pelvic displacement; on the other hand, the abdominal muscles and the hip joint extensors, striving to flex the pelvis on the trunk and thereby producing the opposite kind of pelvic displacement. The first set tends to bring the middle trunk region in front of and the hip region behind the weight line; the other set tends to reverse this weight distribution. Gravity aids whichever set obtains a decided advantage and opposes the other. To the average person it seems at first impossible to make both of these efforts at the same time and in such a way as to straighten the whole spine. When a small measure of success is attained (with assistance, usually), the result is absolute rigidity. Complete success in harmonizing the two kinds of effort hinges on the ability to relax the *lower* erector spinæ while keeping the upper part of this muscle as well as the posterior scapular muscles strongly contracted. When this ability is finally attained the characteristic rigidity of the position disappears to a great extent. For then the action of the glutei and hamstring muscles, which lock the hip joint, may be largely dispensed with, gravity being sufficient to keep this joint in extension. The abdominal muscles, however, must remain contracted to neutralize the partial contraction of the lower erector spinæ which is rarely entirely eliminated, or at any rate to guard the lumbar spine against the effect of sudden contraction of this muscle. Such is apt to occur at any moment, induced by a change of position higher up, e.g., a backward movement of the arms or head.

There need be no fear of excessive contraction of the abdominal muscles on account of the tendency this would have to depress the chest. If the upper erector spinæ, the scapular depressors and other muscles of forced chest expansion remain as active as they should, this does not occur. Any excess of contraction of the abdominal muscles beyond what is needed to keep the lumbar spine straight will then only lead to a retraction of the abdomen. This, to be sure, interferes with the descent of the diaphragm, but as that in turn compels upper and lateral costal breathing, something which most people need to cultivate, it may be considered a gain rather than otherwise.

When the habitual standing position of an individual corresponds to the type described in Section 2, with the hips too far forward, upper spinal curve too long and lower back too straight, excessive lumbar hyperextension is not so apt to occur when efforts are made to straighten the upper back. In such individuals it is of advantage to induce contraction of the whole erector spinæ group, and the resulting moderate increase of hyperextension in the lower back, greater pelvic obliquity and slight backward displacement of the hips represent more favorable weight distribution and are desirable features from an æsthetic, postural and physiological standpoint. But even here the abdominal muscles should be moderately contracted to guard against excessive action of the lower erector spinæ.

The muscular efforts demanded in the gymnastic fundamental standing position and the postural relations, both in the upper and lower part of the body, which result when these efforts are properly coördinated, are of a character to oppose most directly and effectively the unfavorable influences of daily life, and particularly those influences associated with sedentary habits. But aside from direct postural and physiological effects, the repeated and increasingly successful attempts to assume this position and to maintain it for longer and longer periods of time and under varying conditions, are bound to leave their impress on the central nervous system. They train the posture sense, improve the habits of weight distribution, increase the power to inhibit unnecessary or excessive muscular action and so conduce to ease of bearing and economy of effort. All these are essential elements in that subjective control which determines quality and efficiency of bodily action. All represent educational value as truly as the training of habits of logical thinking and effective expression of thought, or of that uprightness of conduct which should underlie all actions and relations in life.

### B.   FOOT PLACINGS AND KNEE BENDINGS.

7.   *Alternate foot placing sideways.*   A movement of one foot at a time directly in the lateral plane, about two foot lengths, weight distributed equally on both feet, and then return to the fundamental position.   The joint mechanism is simple: abduction in both hip joints, starting an instant sooner on the "moving" (left) side than on the "supporting" side.

The principal muscular action is equally simple.   The left femur is moved by its abductors, tensor fasciæ latæ and glutei, while gravity (the body falls to the left as soon as the left foot is lifted), aided by the right tensor fasciæ latæ and glutei, produces the abduction in the right hip joint.   The right hamstring muscles also contract to steady the pelvis on the right femur during the brief period of support on the right foot.   The abdominal muscles and lower erector spinæ on the left side contract at the beginning of the movement, those on the right side at the end—respectively starting and checking the bodily momentum.

The return movement is started by a quick extension in the left ankle which, with the contraction of the right abdominal muscles and lower erector spinæ, gives the body momentum to the right.   This is sufficient to bring the right hip joint to the fundamental, adducted position, but the right adductors also help, especially if the movement is quick.   The left femur is brought to the fundamental position by gravity, aided more or less by the left adductors, according to the speed of the movement.   The right hip joint extensors are again active, as in the first part of the movement.

8.   *Alternate foot placing forward.*   One foot at a time is moved straight ahead about two foot lengths, is firmly planted and receives half of the body weight.

The joint mechanism consists principally of: (1) flexion with slight rotation outward and abduction in the hip joint of the advancing side (left as usual); (2) a corresponding amount of rotation inward and abduction in the hip joint of the supporting side (right); (3) a displacement of the pelvis—tilting forward (increased obliquity) and usually a little rotation to the right, that is, the left side of the pelvis moves forward, the right backward; (4) compensatory changes in the spine—hyperextension and rotation to left.   The displacement of the pelvis with accompanying spinal adjustments takes the place of hyperextension in the right hip joint, and without them the right leg could not be placed (with straight knee) as far behind the erect trunk as the left is moved in front of it. When great care is exercised the only pelvic displacement is a tilting forward. Then the slight rotation and abduction in the hip joints, as well as the spinal rotation, are also absent. Efforts should be made to approach this as nearly as possible. (5) There is a slight, momentary flexion in the left knee joint as the foot is advanced.

The principal active muscles are: (1) The left hip joint flexors and the abdominal muscles. The latter, with the right anterior lower leg muscles, give the body the initial impulse forward. Gravity does the rest. The left tensor fasciæ latæ also contracts, assisting the flexors and producing the slight amount of abduction that may occur. (2) The lower erector spinæ on both sides (left more than the right) contracts sharply just as the left foot strikes the ground, checking the forward momentum of the trunk. (3) The right tensor fasciæ latæ, glutei and hamstring muscles keep the right hip joint locked in extension during the progress of the movement. The two former also resist the tendency to hyperadduction in the right hip joint—a swaying to the right of the pelvis and a "settling" on the right hip—which always occurs when the left foot leaves the ground. Besides, they produce the slight abduction and rotation inward in the right hip joint which may occur. (4) The right quadriceps extensor is active, opposing the tendency of the right knee to bend. The left quadriceps contracts just before the left foot strikes the floor.

The return movement is started by a quick extension in the left ankle and by contraction of the lower erector spinæ on both sides, the right more than the left. The left hip joint extensors, with gravity, bring the left femur back to the fundamental position.

In *oblique foot placings* the features of both the forward and lateral movements are present, but are less pronounced than in either of these.

Alternate foot placings in different directions, while not representing a great amount of general muscular work or very powerful contraction of any particular group, are valuable for the training they give in quick changes of weight distribution, adjustment and balance; in the control of body momentum; and in the localization of movement of the lower extremity as much as possible to the hip joint without too great displacement of the pelvis and trunk. When used in alternation with rhythmical trunk movements they help to keep the latter from becoming "oscillatory," indefinite, incomplete and slovenly, by marking the beginning and end of each movement. They also, when used in this way, contribute to the complexity, variety or difficulty of an exercise.

9. *Standing knee bending.* Of the various movements which may be included under this term the type in which the knees move sideways as far as possible and the heels leave the ground will be assumed. This consists of flexion and abduction with some rotation outward in the hip joint (both sides), flexion in the knee and ankle joints, varying in degree according to whether the knee bending is the customary right angle bend or more (deep knee bending), and, in the ankle, with the height of the heel from the floor.

Gravity is the motor force and the active muscles are the hip joint extensors and abductors—the hamstring muscles, glutei and tensor fasciæ latæ; the quadriceps extensor of the knee; the gastrocnemius, soleus and other extensors of the ankle. The action of these is "eccentric," resisting gravity and determining the speed of the movement. The hip joint abductors are responsible for the "spreading" of the knees. The return movement is accomplished by "concentric" action, that is, shortening of the same muscles. The trunk is kept balanced in the upright position throughout the movement by the contraction of the erector. spinæ against the moderate resistance of the abdominal muscles.

The exercise demands a considerable amount of work on the part of the largest muscles in the body, and when the knee bending is complete these muscles work not only against a greater weight leverage, but also through their whole range. Being well suited to rhythmical repetition it furnishes the most favorable conditions for the increase in size and strength of all those muscles. It also offers fairly great difficulty in keeping the balance, especially in the beginning. This means a lively interplay of all the lower trunk muscles, which adds appreciably to the total amount of work, besides being excellent training in coördination. The erect vertical position of the trunk is favored by the abduction in the hip joint.

10. *Side lunge.* The movement is directly to the side, about three foot lengths, with the knee bent to nearly right angle and pressed sideways as far as possible, the trunk erect and vertical, the shoulders level and "square" to the front. The final position may also be reached by keeping the moving leg straight and bending the knee of the stationary leg.

Assuming the first of the above definitions, the movement consists of flexion, abduction and rotation outward in the hip joint, flexion in the knee and ankle joints of the moving leg (right); abduction (and extension) in the hip joint, extension in the knee and ankle joint of the stationary leg (left). When properly done there is little or no displacement of the pelvis, but in most cases a slight rotation to left and a little tilting to the same

.side are apt to occur, with corresponding twist and bend of the spine to right (convexity to left).

The active muscles are, on the right side: at first, the hip joint flexors and abductors; then, as the right foot strikes the floor, the hip, knee and ankle joint extensors contract, resisting further flexion in these joints by gravity. The hip joint abductors continue active throughout. On the left side the hip joint abductors help to give the body the initial impetus to the left. After the first moment, however, gravity is the chief motor

FIGURE 33

SIDE LUNGE

force, while the left hip joint adductors and the inverters of the left foot contract to keep this foot in firm contact with the floor as the right foot receives the greater part of the body weight. The right abdominal muscles and erector spinæ also contract at the beginning, while the same muscles on the left side check the momentum of the body at the completion of the movement.

The return is accomplished by the quick contraction of the right hip, knee and ankle joint extensors, the left hip joint adductors, the left erector spinæ and abdominal muscles.

### C.   CHARGES AND BACK EXERCISES.

11. *Standing forward charge.* One foot is advanced straight ahead about three foot lengths, toe turned forward, knee bent to nearly right angle. The other foot is either kept firm or allowed to turn on the ball until it is approximately at right angles to the advanced foot, then held in firm contact with the floor. The trunk is kept straight and inclined 45°, *in line with the rear*

*leg.* The plane of the shoulders remains as in the fundamental standing position—"square" to the front. The movement, when properly executed according to this definition, and with the left foot advanced, consists of: (1) flexion and a little abduction in the left hip joint; (2) flexion in the left knee and ankle joints; (3) (extension) rotation outward and slight abduction in the right hip joint; (4) rotation and also a little tilting to right of the pelvis; (5) compensatory twist of the spine to left with a slight lateral bend to the same side (convexity to right).

FIGURE 34
FORWARD CHARGE

The muscular action is very complex, especially if the arms are moved at the same time, as is usually the case. Only the merest outline of the action of the principal muscles will be attempted.

(1) When the left foot is lifted the body is allowed to fall forward, being started in this direction by the right anterior leg and abdominal muscles. The left hip joint flexors—psoas, iliacus, rectus femoris, etc.—raise the left femur; the left knee is flexed by gravity, the quadriceps being relaxed at this stage. (2) When

the foot strikes the ground the left hip, knee and ankle joint extensors contract to check the flexion in these joints. (3) The right hip and knee joints tend to flex as the left foot is advanced, necessitating moderately strong contraction of the right glutei, hamstring muscles and quadriceps. The swinging forward of the right heel means rotation outward in the right hip joint, which is a passive movement produced by the momentum of the trunk. It is resisted and finally checked by the inward rotators— tensor fasciæ latæ, anterior portions of gluteus medius and gluteus minimus. (4) The right foot is kept firmly on the floor by the right hip joint adductors and by the muscles which invert the foot—principally tibialis anticus and posticus. (5) The whole erector spinæ group on each side contracts strongly to keep the spine from being flexed by gravity acting with increasing leverage as the body is inclined. Their action is suddenly increased when the left foot strikes the floor, in order to check the forward momentum of the trunk. (6) The slight bend and considerable twist to the left of the spine, necessary to compensate for the right rotation and inclination of the pelvis, are produced by the stronger contraction of the left back and abdominal muscles and those portions of each which rotate the trunk to the left— left serratus posticus inferior and lower erector spinæ; right serratus posticus superior, semispinales dorsi, multifidus and rotatores spinæ, levatores costarum, right external and left internal oblique abdominal muscles.

The most common faulty tendencies to be resisted in this exercise are: (1) Flexion in the right hip and knee joints and in the whole back due to insufficient contraction of the respective extensors. (2) Raising the heel or outer border of the right foot. (3) Excessive contraction of the lower erector spinæ occurring while the left foot is advancing, leading to hyperextension in the lower back and a vertical position (or even a backward inclination) of the upper trunk. This really reduces the work as well as the difficulty of the exercise. (4) Failure to keep the shoulders "square" to the front, allowing them to rotate to the right so that their plane remains parallel to the plane of the pelvis. This is due to lack of effort or coördination in making the necessary compensatory twisting of the trunk to left. (5) Inclination to left or right of the shoulders, associated with excessive displacements of the pelvis.

12. *Standing oblique charge.* Starting with the feet at right angles, charge diagonally—in the direction the toe points—three foot lengths; knee of advanced leg bent to right angle, rear leg straight, rear foot firmly on floor; trunk inclined about 45°, *in line with the rear leg;* shoulders "square" to the front and bearing the same relation to the trunk as in the standing position

FIGURE 35

OBLIQUE CHARGE

(therefore inclined in the same proportion as the trunk).

The joint mechanism differs but slightly from that of the forward charge. There is moderate abduction and slight rotation outward in both hip joints; the pelvic rotation and lateral tilting and the compensatory twist and bend in the spine are of the same kind as in the forward charge, but less pronounced.

The muscular mechanism is also similar to that of the forward charge, the chief difference being in the stronger action of the hip joint abductors of the advancing leg and the less localized action of the rotators of the trunk. The erector spinæ and abdominal muscles on the side opposite to the charge (the upper side) are most active in sustaining the weight of the trunk and in checking the momentum, which is as much in a lateral as in a forward direction.

The common faults of the final position are: (1) insufficient abduction in the hip joint of the advancing side, shown by the forward position of the knee; (2) flexion in the hip joint of the rear leg; (3) excessive displacements of the pelvis; (4) hyperextension and excessive lateral bends or twists (or both) in the spine.

13. The *toe-support charge position* is similar to the position reached by the forward charge, but instead of one foot (left) being moved forward, the other (right) is moved backward with the ankle extended and only the toe touching the floor (lightly). The stationary forward leg supports practically the whole body weight, which is not displaced in any but a downward direction.

The joint mechanism differs from that of the forward charge (aside from the ankle joint extension) in the absence of rotation outward in the hip joint of the rear leg. This means less pelvic rotation and inclination to right with correspondingly diminished spinal twist and bend to left.

The same muscles are active as in the forward charge, but the sequence and degree of their action are different. The immediate and continued strong contraction of the erector spinæ group on both sides and of the right hip and knee extensors are notable features. The left hip, knee and ankle joint extensors also work harder than in the forward charge, having to sustain the whole body weight throughout.

FIGURE 36

TOE-SUPPORT CHARGE POSITION

Owing to the small amount of support afforded by the rear foot the equilibrium in this position is more unstable than in the forward or the oblique charge. The fact that the body weight is not displaced in any direction (except downward) makes greater speed possible in this movement. Thus, while the joint and muscular mechanism is much the same as in the others, and especially the forward charge, the toe-support charge position and the movement by which it is reached give even greater opportunity than the former for the training of balance, for quick, powerful and delicately adjusted action of all the muscles of the lower trunk and extremity.

14. *The horizontal position on one foot* (horizontal half standing position). Starting from the toe-support charge position, the rear leg is raised and the trunk inclined forward correspondingly, until the line formed by both is horizontal.

The movement consists of additional flexion in the hip joint (and to a much less extent in the knee and ankle joints) of the supporting leg. It is produced chiefly by gravity, aided in the beginning by the anterior lower leg muscles (ankle joint flexors) and the hip joint flexors of the supporting side, the extensors of these joints resisting but being allowed to yield (carefully). The hip joints extensors of the free leg as well as the whole erector spinæ on both sides, and especially the lower portion, contract with utmost intensity to keep the rear leg and trunk in line in the horizontal position. The displacements of pelvis and spine are the same as in the toe-support charge-position, but less pronounced. The action of the back muscles appears to be more equal on the two sides.

The powerful contraction of the lower erector spinæ is apt to cause excessive hyperextension in the lumbar region, which is almost impossible to eliminate. The great difficulty in keeping the balance involves constant and quick yieldings and recoveries on the part of all the muscles of the trunk and lower extremity, and especially of the supporting leg. The muscular work as well as the coördination required by the exercise is therefore very considerable, and the ability to do it well represents a good deal of strength and a high degree of motor control.

15. *Forward bending of trunk* (Fig. 8), already described, is almost entirely flexion at the hips; the thoracic spine is kept extended, the lumbar spine is straightened. The movement is produced by gravity, and the active muscles are the hip joint extensors, the whole erector spinæ group and the posterior scapular muscles. The action of the hip joint extensors and the lower erector spinæ is "eccentric," while the upper erector spinæ and the scapular muscles remain completely contracted.

In *forward-downward bending* (Fig. 9), the flexion in the hip joints and lumbar spine proceeds as far as the extensibility of the hamstring muscles and lower erector spinæ permits. But the upper erector spinæ and posterior scapular muscles should not be allowed to yield.

The return to the fundamental position is accomplished by the "concentric" contraction of the same muscles.

The higher the arms are held in these movements the greater is the weight leverage against which the back muscles have to work. This leverage is also increased in proportion to the inclination of the trunk, the horizontal position representing the maximum. The greater weight leverage, with the added work of the scapular muscles, increases not only the total amount of muscular work but also the difficulty of this type of exercise. The attention is more divided and the extra effort required to keep the arms high and well back induces an even stronger tendency than usual to contract the erector spinæ group as a whole. Or, to put it the other way, the higher the arms are held and the more the trunk is inclined, the more difficult it is to allow the lower erector spinæ to yield without relaxing the upper portion of this group as well as the posterior scapular muscles. When correctly done this type of exercise is therefore very-valuable for the training it gives in localized contraction of the upper back muscles, a most important element in posture education.

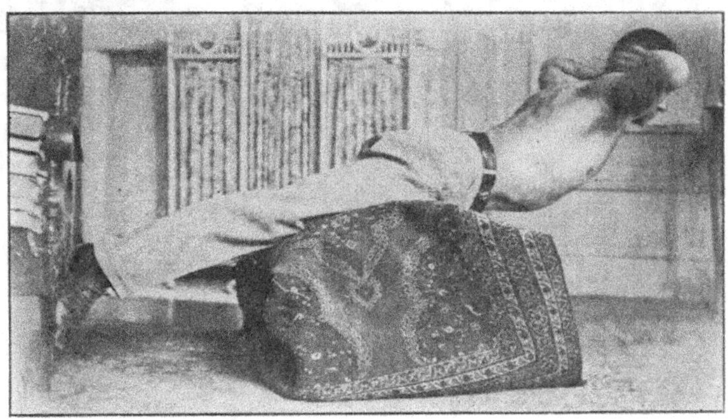

FIGURE 37

PRONE LYING POSITION

16. *The prone lying position.* The body is approximately horizontal, supported under the thighs by a bench or stool; the feet are fixed by another person, by the stall bars, straps or other support.

Gravity, acting with the greatest possible leverage, tends to flex the hip joints and spine and to abduct the scapulæ; the working muscles are therefore the hip joint extensors and all the back muscles, including the scapular adductors and posterior depressors. All contract with utmost vigor, the action of the lower erector spinæ being particularly marked and leading to considerable lumbar hyperextension, which in this case is difficult to avoid.

In *forward bending* from this position the hip joint extensors and lower erector spinæ yield to gravity, but the upper back and posterior scapular (as well as neck) muscles remain contracted, thereby limiting the movement to flexion in the hip joints and lumbar spine. In returning to the starting position the muscles which yielded shorten again until the extension at the hip is complete.

The exercise represents the most powerful type of back movements. Because of the fixation of the legs the localization of the work to the posterior muscles is more absolute and the possibilities for increasing the resistance they have to overcome are greater than in any other type of back exercises. The forcible contraction of the back muscles tends to straighten minor lateral

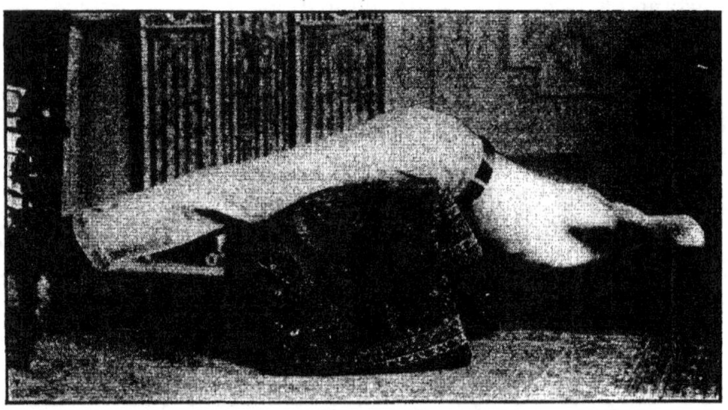

FIGURE 38

FORWARD BENDING FROM PRONE LYING POSITION

deviations of the spine at the time, and by increasing the tone of the muscles to insure greater stability to the spinal column. For these reasons the exercise is used in connection with the treatment of scoliosis. The only objectionable feature is the excessive lumbar hyperextension, but this may be somewhat obviated by refraining from raising the trunk above the horizontal position (or rather beyond the point where it is in line with the legs).

17. *Standing alternate leg raising backward.* The straight leg is displaced directly backward as far as possible without inclining the trunk forward. When the left leg is raised the movement takes place principally in the right hip joint. (1) As the fundamental position implies complete extension of the hip joint, and as the ilio-femoral ligament prevents absolutely any hyperextension, the leg can move backward only by a tilting forward of the pelvis (increasing its obliquity) combined with a tilting to right and a rotation to left on the right femur, in such a way that the left hip is moved backward and upward. The total

pelvic displacement may then be described as flexion, rotation outward and abduction in the right hip joint, the right femur being the fixed segment. (2) At the same time compensatory changes occur in the spine in order to maintain the erect fundamental position of the head, chest, shoulders and upper back. The most conspicuous of these is the lumbar hyperextension, compensating for the forward tilt of the pelvis (flexion in the right hip joint). The lateral tilt of the pelvis (abduction in the right hip joint) is balanced by a bend to the left in the lower spine (convexity to the right), while the backward movement of the left side of the pelvis (rotation outward in the right hip joint) is met by a twist to the right in the whole spine, most pronounced in the lower thoracic region. (3) Finally, the pelvic displacement necessitates a slight abduction and some rotation inward in the left hip joint, if the left leg is to move directly backward with the toe pointed in the same direction.

Muscular mechanism. (1) The left femur is kept extended (against the tendency of gravity to flex it), is abducted and rotated inward by the left hamstring muscles, glutei and tensor fasciæ latæ. (2) The pelvic displacement, i.e., the flexion, abduction, and rotation outward in the right hip joint, is in part produced by the right psoas and iliacus, sartorius, rectus femoris, pectineus, etc., the right tensor fasciæ latæ and glutei; in part by the erector spinæ and abdominal muscles, those on the left side predominating. (3) The last two groups are of course also responsible for the lateral bend of the spine, while the extreme lumbar hyperextension is brought about by contraction of the lower erector spinæ on both sides. (4) The rotation of the pelvis to the left and backward—equivalent to trunk twisting to right—involves also the rotators of the trunk to right, via the right serratus posticus inferior, the right lower erector spinæ and the right internal oblique abdominal muscle; the left semi-spinales dorsi, multifidus spinæ, rotatores spinæ, levatores costarum and the left external oblique abdominal muscle. (5) In keeping the pelvis steady on the right femur there is constant interplay between the right hip joint abductors and adductors, flexors and extensors, in addition to the work many of these have to do as motor muscles. The right lower leg and foot muscles are similarly active.

The movement and the position reached by it are used chiefly as a balance exercise and undeniably answer this purpose very well. The general arching of the back is also apt to induce a forced erect posture in the upper body with good chest expansion, but the excessive lumbar hyperextension which is the main feature of this arching makes its value as a general class exercise at least questionable.

### D.   ABDOMINAL EXERCISES.

18. *Standing alternate leg flinging forward.*   As the name implies, first one leg then the other is moved quickly forward-upward as high as possible and with straight knee.   No position is held at the end of the upward swing, the recoil marking the

FIGURE 39.   LEG FLINGING FORWARD

At the end of the up-swing the leg should be as much above the level of the hip as it is below in the figure.

beginning of the return movement.   At the changes from one leg to the other, however, the fundamental position is held for a moment.   The head and upper back should not be allowed to bend forward as the leg rises, and the tendency to bend the knee of the supporting leg should be resisted.   The left leg will be assumed to be the moving leg.

The joint mechanism of this movement involves (1) as much flexion in the left hip joint as the length and elasticity of the left hamstring muscles permit; (2) flexion of the pelvis on the trunk, that is, a tilting of the pelvis to a more horizontal position.   This can be done only by a straightening of the lumbar spine and by compensatory movements in the right hip and knee joints; (3) if the extension in both hip joints is complete at the outset, there can be no further movement in the right joint to allow the flexion of the pelvis.   If it is not, the pelvis moves on the right femur until the ilio-femoral ligament is tense and the extension in the right hip joint is complete.   Any further flexion of the pelvis on the trunk necessitates flexion in the right knee joint, and this nearly always occurs to a greater or less extent, if the leg flinging is vigorous enough to bring the foot above waist level.   (4) As soon as the left foot leaves the ground the weight which it supported must be transferred to the right foot.   This is done by a slight shifting of the pelvis to the right, and involves a corresponding amount of adduction or rather hyperadduction in the right hip joint.

The muscles active in the movement are (1) the left hip joint flexors, principally the psoas, iliacus and rectus femoris; (2) the abdominal muscles. These always contract whenever the hip joint flexors, even on one side, are active. The functional association between the two sets is analogous to that between the deltoid and supraspinatus on one hand, the trapezius and serratus magnus on the other. The hip joint flexors in their efforts to draw the femur forward-upward also tend to tip the pelvis forward, that is, to increase its obliquity. The abdominal muscles do just the opposite, viz., flex the pelvis on the trunk, making its plane approach nearer the horizontal. They are therefore fixators of the pelvis against the pull of the hip joint flexors. In this capacity the abdominal muscles may be said to do more than their duty: they pull the anterior margin of the pelvis upward, and so increase the range of movement of the femur in an upward direction. This tilting of the pelvis begins long before the limit of flexion in the hip joint has been reached. Another way of looking at it is to consider the abdominal muscles and the hip joint flexors parts of one system or muscular mechanism serving the purpose of flexing the two segments—pelvis and femur—on the trunk and always working together in the accomplishment of this purpose. (3) In the effort to flex the pelvis on the trunk the abdominal muscles are aided by the hip joint extensors—principally the gluteus maximus and the hamstring muscles. Those on the right side contract actively, while those on the left side are being subjected to strong tension, owing to the flexion of the left hip joint while the left knee is kept extended, and thereby exert a powerful pull on the posterior portions of the pelvis. When, through the united action of all, the pelvis has been flexed on the trunk (and extended on the right femur) until no further movement in the right hip joint can take place (the ilio-femoral ligament being stretched), continued action of the abdominal muscles and hip joint extensors, aided by the momentum of the left leg and by gravity, will flex the right knee joint (the quadriceps, strongly contracted from the beginning, has to yield a little). This allows a forward movement of the right femur and a corresponding amount of additional flexion of the pelvis on the trunk. (4) In the slight movement of the pelvis to the right when the left foot leaves the ground the abductors of the right hip joint—glutei and tensor fasciæ latæ—contract, but yield to gravity until equilibrium on the right foot has been established. After that, they, as well as the adductors, maintain static contraction, steadying the pelvis on the femur and preventing or reducing lateral swaying. The action of the right extensors against the ilio-femoral ligament (and flexor muscles), already described as aiding in the flexion of the pelvis on the trunk, prevents or checks antero-posterior oscillations.

The main features of this exercise may be summed up as follows: (1) Extreme stretching of the hamstring muscles and other structures on the posterior aspect of the thigh and knee of the moving side in order to attain as complete flexion in the hip joint as possible with straight knee. (2) Forced complete extension in the hip joint of the supporting side. (3) Considerable flexion of the pelvis on the trunk, associated with forced flexion in one hip joint and leading to complete extension in the other. (4) Straightening and even reversal of the lumbar curve, occurring as an essential part of flexion of the pelvis on the trunk. (5) Vigorous contraction of the abdominal muscles, always induced by efforts to flex the hip joint. (6) Prompt, vigorous and orderly interplay of the flexors and extensors, abductors and adductors of the hip joint on the supporting side involved in the redistribution of weight at the change from one foot to the other and in maintaining the balance during the progress of the movement. (7) Lastly, the yielding and stretching of the lower erector spinæ, necessary in the flexion of the lumbar spine, while the upper erector spinæ and the posterior scapular muscles remain in complete contraction, keeping the upper part of the body erect under conditions of unusual difficulty.

19. *Standing alternate knee upward bending* is like alternate leg flinging forward in all respects except that the knee on the moving side is flexed at the same time and in the same proportion as the hip joint on that side. This reduces the passive tension on the hamstring muscles of that side to a minimum and so allows complete flexion in the hip joint, limited only by the contact of the thigh with the abdomen. When the movement is done slowly and the position is held as a balance exercise, the right angle flexion at hip and knee is customary. The main object is then to cultivate quick and orderly interplay between the flexors and extensors, abductors and adductors of the hip joint, and of the muscles of the lower leg which

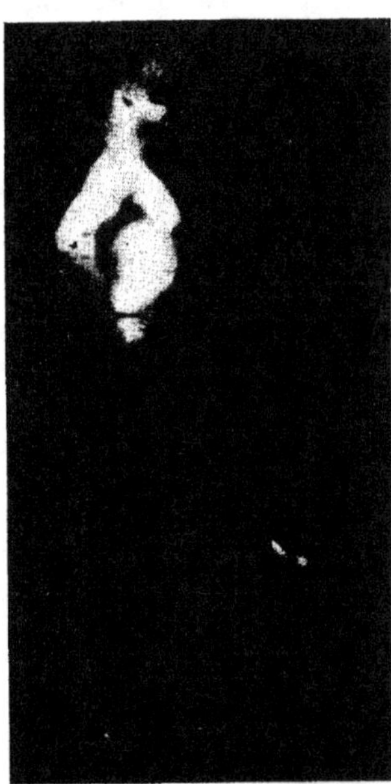

FIGURE 40. ALTERNATE KNEE UPWARD BENDING

At the end of the up-stroke the knee should be close to the chest.

steady the ankle joint, all on the supporting side, as well as of all the lower trunk muscles, in order to maintain a steady balance on one foot. But the action of the abdominal muscles and the resulting flexion of the pelvis on the trunk through straightening of the-lumbar spine still remain prominent features of the exercise.

20. *Knee upward bending, and leg raising from the hanging position.* When one leg is moved at a time the mechanism of these, as regards the lower body, is the same as in the corresponding movements from the standing position. But the hanging position eliminates the balance element, insures a straight upper back, fixes the chest in an expanded position and so makes possible more energetic action of the abdominal muscles and hip joint flexors of the moving side.

*When both legs are raised* (straight) the work of the hip joint flexors and abdominal muscles is much increased owing to the greater weight leverage as well as to the increased resistance offered by the hamstring muscles on both sides. The range of flexion of the pelvis on the trunk is somewhat greater than when one leg is raised, as the limitation involved in keeping one hip joint extended is absent.

*In double knee upward bending* the abdominal muscles and hip joint flexors have less weight to lift and encounter less resistance from the hamstring muscles. Because of the latter, greater flexion of the femur on the pelvis and of the pelvis on the trunk is possible, and the motor muscles are therefore able to shorten more completely. This means as complete flexion in the lumbar spine as this region is capable of. The hanging position induces a fairly straight upper thoracic spine and good chest expansion. Here, then, all conditions are favorable for improving the postural relations of the whole trunk, including the shoulder and hip regions. Most of the muscles responsible for the maintenance of good posture in the different regions are given opportunity to contract through their whole range and against a considerable resistance. In the case of the scapular depressors, rotators downward and adductors, while they are not shortened completely, their contraction is sustained for some time. The antagonistic structures, muscular and fibrous, are stretched. The mobility in the joints of the spine, chest and shoulder girdle, as well as in the shoulder joint proper, is cultivated in directions in which it tends to become limited through lack of opportunity or necessity for such extreme movements in the ordinary activities of daily life. This type of exercise is also one of the most effective for increasing the strength and tone of the abdominal muscles, as well as for reducing, or at least retarding, the accumulation of adipose tissue so frequently associated with relaxed abdominal walls in persons of sedentary habits. At the same time the abdominal muscles work under mechanical conditions entirely different from those of the standing position, such as fixation of chest, instead of pelvis, changed relation to gravity, association with the hip joint flexors instead of the extensors. Therefore exercises of this type fail to give much training in the kind of coördination, weight distribution and balance necessary for a good carriage in the lower part of the body. These are best acquired through the practice of exercises done from the fundamental standing position.

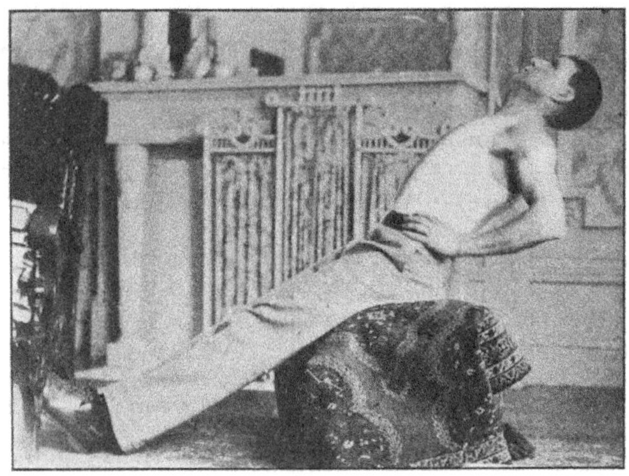

FIGURE 41

OPPOSITE SITTING BACKWARD LEANING OF THE TRUNK

21. *Opposite sitting backward leaning of the trunk.* From the sitting position with knees straight and feet fixed (or, if the knees are bent, with thighs fixed), the trunk is inclined backward a varying amount. The movement should be done only at the hips (extension), without any lumbar hyperextension. The upper back is kept straight, the head well back and the chest expanded.

The extension in the hip joint is caused by gravity and is resisted by the hip joint flexors—psoas and iliacus, sartorius, pectineus, etc. The first effect of their contraction is to fix the pelvis and lower lumbar spine, thereby tending to localize the movement to the upper lumbar and lower thoracic spine. This tendency is favored from the outset by the strong contraction of the lower erector spinæ, induced by efforts to keep the upper back straight; also by the direct forward pull of the psoas on the lumbar vertebræ, and by gravity. The proper localization of the movement to (extension in) the hip joint demands, therefore, in the first place prompt and vigorous contraction of the abdominal muscles to neutralize excessive action of the lower erector spinæ and the ilio-psoas, and to resist gravity; secondly, ability to allow the psoas and other hip joint flexors to yield; finally, ability to relax, partly at least, the lower erector spinæ, without inducing relaxation of the upper portions of this group and the posterior scapular muscles. If these upper back (and posterior neck) muscles fail to act, the effect of the pull of the abdominal muscles and the associated contraction of the pectorals and anterior neck muscles will be to depress the chest, to flex the upper back, neck and head, to draw the shoulders forward and upward—literally to curl up the upper part of the body. This, by reducing the weight leverage and giving the abdominal muscles the advantage, makes the movement easier, and is the most common fault in the execution.

To induce the right kind of muscular effort and so insure proper localization of the movement it is of advantage, at first, to start with abdomen retracted, then to move the head backward (with chin drawn in), at the same time taking a deep breath. It is well not to allow the movement to proceed far enough to induce excessive contraction of the anterior muscles, with visible tremors, as this nearly always leads to involuntary relaxation of the upper back muscles. When properly done, that is, from the hips, with the whole back straight, the chest expanded and the head in fundamental position, the movement is not only one of the most powerful abdominal exercises, but also gives excellent training in the kind of muscular control required for a good carriage of both the upper and lower part of the body.

22. *Leg raising from the lying position.* Lying flat on the back, with hands "behind" the neck or stretched out "above" the head, the legs are raised, with straight knees, to the vertical position. The movement consists of flexion in the hip joint, supplemented by flexion of the pelvis on the trunk—in other words, flexion in the lower spine. The latter is preceded, during the first part of the movement, by increased lumbar hyperextension associated with a slight forward tilting of the pelvis.

The active muscles are the hip joint flexors—psoas, iliacus, rectus femoris, etc., and the abdominal muscles. As in "Opposite sitting backward leaning of trunk" the first effect of the contraction of the hip joint flexors, and particularly of the psoas-iliacus, is a tendency to tilt the pelvis forward (increase its obliquity), shown by the increased arching "forward" of the lower spine. This is soon checked and reversed by the contraction of the abdominal muscles. It may even be entirely avoided if these muscles are brought into strong action at the outset and are aided for a brief moment by the hip joint extensors.

To prevent any depression of the chest by the pull of the abdominal muscles it is of advantage to take a deep breath at the beginning of the

FIGURE 42

LEG RAISING FROM THE LYING POSITION

movement, exhale when the vertical position of the legs has been reached, then inhale again as the legs are lowered. This, however, increases the tendency to arch the lower back during the first stage of the rise and the last stage of the return. In some cases there is difficulty in keeping the head and arms in contact with the floor during these stages, when the weight leverage is greatest. This may be obviated by grasping some solid object.

23. *The prone falling position.* (Front leaning rest, Fig. 24.) The muscular action in the upper trunk and shoulder region has already been described. In the lower part of the body gravity tends to flex the knees, to keep the hip joints extended and to hyperextend the lumbar spine. This necessitates contraction of the quadriceps extensor and the abdominal muscles. Associated action of the hip joint flexors, often excessive, is apt to cause a bend at the hips. When this is the case the hip joint extensors must also be brought into action. The hip joint is then effectually locked and the full force of the abdominal muscles can be brought to bear on the lower spine in a way to prevent hyperextension. After the proper muscular control has been acquired excessive action of the hip joint flexors does not occur and action of the

extensors is therefore not necessary, gravity being sufficient to keep the hip joint extended.

### E.   LATERAL TRUNK EXERCISES.

24. *Standing alternate leg flinging sideways.* The quick extreme movement of the straight leg, say the left, directly in the lateral plane, will be assumed. The upper trunk remains erect, the shoulders level. The main joint mechanism is as follows: (1) extreme abduction in the left hip joint; (2) a tilting of the pelvis to the right, the crest of the left ilium being the highest point (this movement takes place in the right hip joint and is abduction in this joint, the right femur being the fixed, and the pelvis the moving segment); (3) a compensatory lateral bend of the spine, convexity to right, most pronounced in the lumbar region.

The principal muscles concerned in producing the movement and keeping the balance are: (1) The abductors of the left hip joint— tensor fasciæ latæ, glutei; (2) the abductors of the right hip joint, assisting in tilting the pelvis; (3) the flexors and extensors of the right hip joint, keeping the pelvis steady on the right femur as regards the antero-posterior plane; (4) the abdominal muscles and lower erector spinæ on the left side, being the chief factors in the tilting of the pelvis and in producing the lateral bend of the spine.

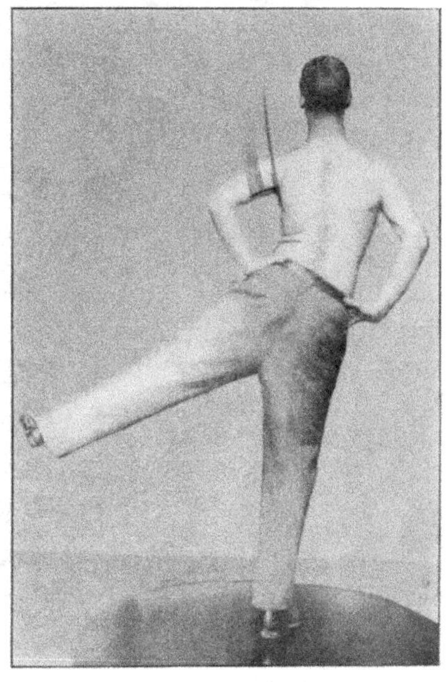

FIGURE 43.   LEG RAISING SIDEWAYS

In a quick flinging the leg should be almost on a level with the hip at the end of the up-swing.

Their contraction is preceded by a momentary contraction of the corresponding muscles on the right side to check the displacement of the hips and lower trunk to right, necessary to balance the body on the right foot; (5) the right knee extensors are also strongly active, the left more moderately. The same is true of the lower leg (and foot) muscles of the respective sides.

The alternate movement is a good all-round exercise with the features of waist or lateral trunk movements predominating. It is capable of being done with good, erect posture in the upper part of the body, demands quick, successive weight adjustment and so offers at least moderate difficulty in keeping the balance. This may be increased by doing the exercise slowly, or by holding the abducted position of the leg a varying length of time.

25. *Standing side-bending of trunk* (to right). When correctly and completely done the exercise involves the whole range of lateral movement in the thoracic and lumbar spine and includes also a displacement of the pelvis to the left, equivalent to abduction in the right hip joint and adduction in the left. The plane of the shoulders should not be disturbed; that is, the movement should be directly to the side, without twisting or forward bending in the upper spine, backward bending in the lower, or flexion at the hips.

FIGURE 44
SIDE-BENDING OF TRUNK

The abdominal muscles, lower erector spinæ and hip joint abductors on the right side contract for an instant at the beginning. After that gravity is the motor force and the same muscles on the left side act "eccentrically," regulating the speed and determining the plane of the movement. Then, by shortening, they raise the trunk to the fundamental position. The hip joint extensors are moderately active throughout. The upper erector spinæ and posterior scapular muscles are also in a state of greater activity than in the erect position, as the changes in weight distribution disturb their ordinary relations. The higher the arms are held the more this is the case.

26. *Side-bending from the side-lying position.* The support is placed under one thigh, say the right, and the feet are fixed. The body should be approximately horizontal, bent a little to the left (upward), the plane of the shoulders and hips vertical, the hip and knee joints extended. The movement from this posi_ tion—side-bending to right—is distributed over the whole spine and continues until the head is near the floor.

FIGURE 45
SIDE-BENDING FROM THE SIDE-LYING POSITION

The principal muscles active in maintaining the position against gravity are the same as in "standing side-bending," viz., the abdominal muscles, the erector spinæ and its upper prolongations, and the hip joint abductors, all on the left side; also the hip and knee joint extensors on both sides. During the bending these muscles while yielding to gravity are nevertheless in strong action ("eccentric"), guiding the movement in the lateral plane. During the return movement they have to contract with extreme vigor owing to the great weight leverage. This, with the very considerable amount of work required of the scapular adduc- tors and depressors, makes the exercise one of the most powerful of the lateral trunk movements.

27. *Side falling position* (side leaning rest). The straight and rigid body, with the (left) side toward the floor is supported on the left hand and foot. The left shoulder joint is in a position

of incomplete abduction, the left scapula at best is slightly rotated upward, but its position varies according to the strength and control of the scapular muscles possessed by the performer.  The rest of the body should be as nearly as possible in the fundamental position.

Gravity tends to produce flexion in the left elbow, adduction in the left shoulder joint, elevation with some adduction and rotation downward of the left scapula, a bend to right in the spine (convexity to left), abduction in the right hip joint, adduction in the left.  There is also a tendency to flexion in both hip joints and to forward bending of the upper spine.

The principal active muscles are: the left triceps; the left shoulder joint abductors—deltoid, supraspinatus and long head of biceps; all the left scapular muscles, and especially the lower serratus magnus; the left erector spinæ and abdominal muscles; the left hip joint abductors and the right adductors; also the hip joint extensors on both sides.  The upper erector spinæ and posterior neck muscles are active on both sides, the right more than the left.  There is some difficulty, at first, in keeping the body from rolling over forward or backward.  The balance is maintained by interplay between the oblique abdominal and back muscles which rotate the trunk to right and left respectively, as well as between the left pectorals and serratus magnus on one hand and the left latissimus, posterior deltoid, trapezius and rhomboids on the other.

The total muscular work and the difficulty in keeping the balance may be increased progressively by moving the free (right) arm to higher levels, and still more·by raising the right leg.

28.  *Side holding* (left side up).  Grasping the stall bars or similar apparatus with the hands about three or four feet apart, the left directly above the right (palms facing each other), the body is swung out sideways to an approximately horizontal position and held there as long as the strength of the performer permits.  Or the exercise may be done as a rhythmical movement, without attempting to hold the position at the end of the up-swing. In either case the muscular action is of the same kind, differing only in degree.  The horizontal position, representing the maximum effort, will be assumed for purposes of analysis.

Both shoulder joints are then abducted and both scapulæ rotated upward.  Gravity tends to carry the abduction in the left shoulder joint and the rotation upward of the left scapula still further, while on the right side the opposite tendency prevails. The spine tends to bend to right (convexity to left), while in the hip joints there is tendency to adduction in the left, abduction in the right and flexion in both.

The muscles which produce the movement, hold the position and resist in the return are: (1) the left shoulder joint adductors —-pectoralis major, latissimus and teres major; (2) the downward rotators and depressors of the left scapula—rhomboids, lower trapezius and pectoralis minor; (3) the right shoulder joint abductors—deltoid, supraspinatus and long head of biceps; (4) the upward rotators of the right scapula—serratus magnus and trapezius (the depressors of the right scapulæ are also active ); (5) the left abdominal muscles and erector spinæ; (6) the left tensor fasciæ latæ and the right hip joint adductors; (7) the glutei and hamstring muscles on both sides. Besides these, the right triceps is strongly active opposing the tendency of gravity to flex the right elbow. The left triceps also has to contract, as the strong pull of the left shoulder joint adductors and the associated contraction of the left biceps tend to flex the left elbow. The body is kept from swinging forward or backward (toward the wall) by timely contraction of all the upper back and posterior shoulder muscles, or the abdominal and pectoral muscles, respectively.

At the beginning of the movement, with the trunk bent to the right and the left arm elevated, the left side of the chest is forcibly expanded. During the ascent, and particularly when the body is in or near the horizontal position, the pull of the left shoulder joint adductors and the scapular depressors on both sides makes the chest expansion general.

The exercise demands considerable strength and coördination, but if the momentum is properly managed by swinging the left leg first toward the wall and then outward, it is not as severe nor as difficult as might at first appear. Keeping the arms absolutely rigid and the right shoulder low throughout are also essential factors in successful performance.

29. *Standing alternate trunk twisting.* As this is most commonly done, little or no restriction is demanded as to where the movement is to take place. It often includes the cervical, as well as the thoracic and lumbar regions of the spine, and nearly always rotation of the pelvis. The latter involves movements of opposite character in all the joints of the two lower extremities. If the twisting is to left, there is flexion, rotation inward and adduction in the left hip joint, extension, rotation outward and abduction in the right; flexion in the right knee and ankle joints, a slight extension in the left; eversion of the right foot, inversion of the left.

Here the "pure" type of trunk twisting will be assumed. This may be defined as taking place entirely above the hips, with the head remaining immovable relative to the shoulders. Such a movement employs the whole range of rotation in the thoracic spine, as well as the small amount possible in the lumbar region, while the cervical spine, the pelvis, the hip, knee and ankle joints remain fixed in the fundamental position by conscious muscular effort. When thus restricted the movement rarely exceeds 45°.

Besides the oblique abdominal and back muscles directly concerned in the production of the movement (enumerated several times in connection with movements previously described, e.g., in forward charge, page 106) practically all the muscles of the hip region and lower extremities, including the inverters of the feet, contract in the effort to fix the pelvis and legs. The scapular adductors and posterior depressors on both sides are also required to act vigorously to resist the strong tendency to independent displacements of the shoulders.

The localized movement, especially when done quickly and when the position reached by it is held a moment, although of smaller range, demands more general and more vigorous muscular work, and a great deal more coördination, than the more extensive, less localized type in which no attempt is made to keep the hips immovable. In the former the action of the abdominal muscles is particularly marked, so much, in fact, that the breathing, both diaphragmatic and costal, may be somewhat impeded. The arches of the feet are subjected to less strain, owing to the strong contraction of the tibialis anticus and posticus, as well as of the plantar muscles, all associated with the effort to fix the legs and pelvis. After some practice the exercise may, however, be properly localized without much muscular effort below the hips, at least when done slowly.

30. *Walking, running and jumping.* For the mechanics of locomotion the reader is referred to the writings of those investigators who have made a detailed study of the subject—Marey, Demeny, Fisher, Fuchs and others. (See Bibliography.) Here only the most obvious features of the joint and muscular mechanism of these forms of movement will be considered.

*Walking.* Starting at the point when the left foot leaves the ground, with the left hip, knee and ankle joint more or less extended, the sequence of movements is about as follows: (1) Flexion and slight rotation outward in the left hip joint and flexion in the left knee joint. This is probably chiefly a passive movement (the whole leg acting as a jointed pendulum), aided perhaps by a slight contraction of the hip joint flexors and outward rotators—psoas and iliacus, rectus femoris, sartorius, pectineus, etc., and of the knee joint flexors. The ankle joint has to be slightly flexed by muscular action in order to allow the toe to clear the ground. (2) In the meanwhile, extension and slight rotation inward have taken place in the right hip joint, as well as some adduction, shown by the swaying of the hips to right when the right leg receives the weight. The principal active muscles here are the glutei, tensor fasciæ latæ and hamstring muscles. (3) The right knee joint may flex somewhat when the leg receives the weight, but this is checked, and the joint more or less extended by the contraction of the quadriceps. (4) The right ankle joint has been flexed, partly by the momentum of the body, partly by active contraction of the anterior lower leg muscles. (5) The pelvis, besides being displaced to the right in the settling of the weight on the right hip (equivalent to adduction in the right hip joint) has also rotated to the right on the right femur, so that the left hip is a little in advance of the right when the left foot strikes the ground. This rotation of the pelvis may also be expressed in terms of rotation inward in the right hip joint and necessitates the outward rotation in the left hip joint mentioned above. (6) When the right hip joint has reached complete extension a further movement of the body in front of the right leg involves a forward inclination of the pelvis (increase of its obliquity). (7) The forward inclination and rotation to the right of the pelvis call for compensatory hyperextension and twisting to left of the spine, in order to keep the upper trunk erect and the plane of the shoulders "square" to the front. The forward swing of the right arm and the backward swing of the left, if extensive, may even induce a change in plane of the shoulders opposite to that of the hips, so that the right shoulder is slightly in front of the left. This makes the left twist of the spine more pronounced. Often there is also a depression of the left shoulder, involving a bend to left (convexity to right) of the spine. The erector spinæ group and the abdominal muscles are responsible for these adjustments, the muscles on the right side in the case of the former being most active, while in the case of the latter the right external and left internal oblique work together. The swaying to right of the pelvis is necessary in the transfer of the weight to the right foot, and involves action, for the purpose of support, of the right abdominal and erector spinæ muscles, as well as of the right hip joint abductors.

The different phases of each stride in walking vary considerably with the frequency and length of the stride. Thus, for example, in slow sauntering the knee of the advancing leg is completely extended when the foot strikes the ground, while in some forms of rapid walking it may remain partly flexed at that moment. In the so-called flexion gait, cultivated or natural, it is not completely extended at any time. The lateral oscillation and rotation of the pelvis, and the compensatory movements of spine, shoulders and arms, are also subject to variations with individual peculiarities of structure and habits of movement. It is these individual variations in the elements of the complete step that make the gait of each individual characteristic, and they indicate, perhaps better than any other single form of movement, the degree of subjective motor control and the general motor habits of the individual.  In gymnastic marching, and especially in certain forms of balance marching and steps, it is possible to analyze, to some extent, these elements and by emphasizing some or "toning down" others, to improve the gait.  Turning up the toe of the advancing foot excessively, may be helped by practicing a step in which the ball of the foot strikes the floor first, or in which the sole remains parallel to the floor; excessive lateral sway and rotation of the pelvis, or the compensatory swinging and depression of the shoulders, may be made less pronounced by balance marching in which these movements of the pelvis and shoulders are reduced to a minimum.  All these exercises tend to improve the individual's sense of balance, habits of weight distribution and localization of movement, and if supplemented by constant attention and persistent application outside of the gymnasium, may be expected to produce appreciable results in the way of permanent improvement of the gait.

*Running.*  This form of locomotion, like walking, presents so many different varieties that it would be difficult to describe a typical style.  It differs from walking essentially in that the body leaves the ground entirely at each step, and in that the excursions of the legs and the oscillations of the pelvis and shoulders are, in general, more extensive.  In fast running practically all the muscles of the body are in action, most pronounced in the case of the extensors of the hip, knee and ankle, the flexors of the hip, and the erector spinæ and abdominal muscles.

*Jumping.*  Here again there are a number of styles or types, differing widely in detail, from the simple gymnastic jump, in which the trunk remains vertical and facing forward, to the very complex forms of running high jump used in athletic competition, in which the trunk is inclined backward and a more or less sharp or complete turn is executed at the moment of passing the bar.

In all forms, however, the spring consists of a preliminary flexion of the knee, hip and ankle joints of one side, followed by a quick extension in these joints, and a flexion in the hip joint and sometimes the knee joint of the other side.  This is in turn followed by flexion in the joints of the springing leg, accompanied or not, as the case may be, by a twist, or turn, of the whole body toward the side of this leg.

Jumping, even more than running, involves very general muscular action, the back, hip, knee and ankle extensors, the hip joint flexors and the abdominal muscles being the principal groups.  The action is of a more sudden and extreme character and more delicately adjusted, demanding a relatively higher degree of coördination. Here judgment of distance and momentum, correct timing and sequence of effort are perhaps more essential for successful performance than in any other form of movement. But because of the intermittent and violent character of the muscular work, jumping, from a physiological standpoint, is not as useful a general exercise as running.

# SUMMARY.

In the introduction the general character of gymnastics was contrasted with that of the other principal forms of exercise used as agents in physical education. The effectiveness of gymnastics in certain directions, such as equalizing growth and development, favoring correct anatomical relations and increasing the functional activity of the great vital organs, was assumed to be generally recognized. It was further claimed that gymnastics of the right kind may be made one of the most effective agents in motor education, and particularly in that phase which has to do with the carriage and management of the parts of the body with reference to each other, and of the body as a whole with reference to external forces and things in a purely subjective manner, such as its position in space, its relation and adjustment to gravity, inertia and momentum—involving weight distribution and balance; direction, speed and accuracy of movement; timing and proper distribution of effort. The degree and quality of this subjective motor control are suggested by such terms as bearing, poise, physical presence, grace, agility. Its value as a means of expression, as a factor in the social relations of life and as a basis for physical efficiency is variously estimated and on the whole probably underrated.

In the analysis of the gymnastic exercises it was frequently pointed out how apparently slight differences in the definition of an exercise, or emphasis on some particular feature, may change it from an easy insignificant movement, requiring relatively slight expenditure of energy and offering little or no difficulty of coördination, to one calling for vigorous, discriminating, well-coördinated muscular efforts, usually of a kind tending directly or indirectly to preserve erect carriage and to improve postural relations. Indeed, conscious effort to maintain good posture under all conditions is (or should be) one of the chief characteristics of gymnastic movements. It is one of the most important elements of that definiteness of detail which distinguishes the gymnastic movement from its non-gymnastic prototype, and which makes the former so much more difficult than the latter.

1. *Definiteness of gymnastic exercises.* If the objects of gymnastics are to include such things as refinement of subjective motor control and improvement of postural relations, these objects can hardly be attained in any marked degree by the practice of vague, ill-defined, relatively complex movements, executed in a listless, haphazard, slovenly or at best mechanical, oscillatory

manner. It is not reasonable to expect that work which does not call for concentration of attention and effort, for discrimination and judgment, shall cultivate these powers and qualities in the doer and lead to habits of efficient action. To do this the gymnastic movements must be selected, defined and presented in a way to focus attention, to exercise the discriminative and inhibitive powers, and to elicit vigorous, clean-cut, well-adjusted motor reactions. Moreover, to suit the needs of the majority they must embody certain essential features, relating to the carriage of the body, the quantity, kind, variety, distribution and continuity of the muscular work. To be capable of presentation to an execution in unison by a number of individuals, and in a manner to bring out their full effects, they must be relatively simple, or if complex, must be capable of subdivision into simpler elements, each of which may be presented and executed as a complete movement. They must be sharply defined in every detail, such as plane or direction, kind, extent and speed of movement; parts of the body involved; the exact relation of these parts in the position reached by the movement; relative length of time spent in moving and in holding the position—rhythm; the muscles or groups of muscles brought into action and the character of their action. With this exactness of definition there must be insistence on promptness, precision and unison in the execution. Whether the exercises are done singly on command or repeated rhythmically, each movement (or each part of a compound or alternating movement) must be completed, and the position marking its completion held for a brief space of time, before the return, or the next part, is begun. This involves checking momentum and overcoming inertia at every point, introduces the element of balance and redistribution of weight more frequently or more prominently, compels more complete, powerful and varied muscular action, gives the pupil an opportunity to note and understand what he is doing, and the teacher a chance to help him, if necessary. On the degree of definiteness in all these respects depends, to a great extent, the effectiveness of gymnastic exercises in the directions already indicated. Lacking this, gymnastic work is justified only on grounds of hygienic necessity, is merely a rather uninteresting, monotonous way of getting muscular exercise when nothing more attractive is available.

This element of definiteness in gymnastic movements, on which their special effectiveness so largely depends, involves a number of closely related factors, some of the most important of which are: localization of movement, localization of muscular contraction, fixation, the supporting function of muscles.

2. *Localization of movement.* With this is meant the confinement of movement to certain specified regions, the limitation

of the number of segments or joints taking part, and usually the emphasis or completeness of one kind of movement to the exclusion of all others. As regards joint mechanism, therefore, localization is equivalent to simplicity and definiteness of movement. Thus, for example, the gymnastic movement forward bending of trunk takes place chiefly in the hip joints, while the spine, chest and shoulder girdle remain in fundamental position; in trunk twisting the spine is the region of localization, while the pelvis and lower extremities remain immovable; in arm bending the completeness of flexion in the elbow and of rotation outward in the shoulder joint, with a minimum amount of abduction or hyperextension in the shoulder joint and displacement of the scapula, are the essential features.

The muscular action in localized movements differs from that in non-localized movements chiefly in two ways, the prominence of the one or the other depending upon the nature of the movement and on the degree of muscular control possessed by the individual. (1) Movement may be localized by inhibiting the action of all muscles not directly concerned, that is, by localizing the muscular action to those groups only which pull directly on the segments involved. (2) By neutralizing the effect of adventitious or associated muscular action, of gravity, momentum and inertia through static action of muscles antagonistic to these forces, thereby insuring fixation of all parts which it is desired to exclude from the movement.

3. *Localization of muscular contraction.* Most movements are produced by combined or associated action of many muscles. This association or functional grouping of muscles may serve the purpose of producing any one of several kinds of movements possible in one joint, or it may be of a more general character, leading to movement of the same kind in several joints. The combined action of the latissimus, teres major and pectoralis major in producing adduction in the shoulder joint is an example of the first kind of grouping; the associated action of the hip joint flexors and the abdominal muscles in raising the leg forward is a good example of the second. When it is desired to move a segment through a wide range, or against considerable resistance, or very quickly, the tendency is always to distribute the movement over many joints and to bring into action a great number of associated muscle groups. But even in movements of moderate extent, speed and power this tendency to distribution is strong. Moderate contraction of many muscles seems easier than powerful contraction of a few, even if the total expenditure of energy is greater in the long run. At any rate this kind of muscular action is apt to lead to excessive, cumbersome and ill-adjusted movement.

Localization of muscular contraction is the limitation of the number of muscles or groups taking part in the production of a given movement. It implies inhibition of unnecessary, induced or associated muscular action, often involves disassociation of large, fundamental group associations, and is thus a determining factor in the number, variety and accuracy of coördinated movements. The power of localized muscular action varies in individuals and in different parts of the body. In the trunk it is never very great, but it may be increased by training./ One way to increase this power is by the practice of definite gymnastic exercises, in which the movements are localized through fixation by conscious muscular effort of all parts not directly concerned (see fixation). This, for one thing, gives opportunity for complete and vigorous contraction of the motor muscles proper. It also teaches the individual to perceive more clearly the different elements of complex movements, to appreciate finer distinctions and to "find" more readily the right kind and degree of muscular action needed in these combinations. By means of the keener kinesthetic sense cultivated in this way he is able, after a while, to inhibit more perfectly the unnecessary muscular contractions induced through habitual association of groups belonging to the same general system, and to reduce correspondingly the amount of muscular work necessary for purposes of fixation. The extent to which all unnecessary muscular action can be thus eliminated, represents the degree of power of localized muscular contraction, and this, in the last analysis, is the basis of skill, grace and economy of effort. The whole process may be summarized by the statement made in the introductory part, that by the practice of definite, localized gymnastic exercises, the inhibition of unnecessary elements in movement becomes a central rather than a peripheral affair.

4. *Fixation.* Aside from the instinctive tendency to distribute movement over large areas through the induced contraction of muscles habitually associated, localization of movement is made difficult by the mechanical influence of many muscles on other parts than those to which they are attached. The majority of the larger muscles, and especially those of the trunk, play over several joints and by their contraction or tension produce or modify movement, not only of the segments to which they are attached but of intervening segments as well. Sometimes, through passive tension of other muscles, or through mechanical fixation of distant points (hands or feet), movement may be produced even in parts which lie beyond those on which the muscles pull directly. For example, in arm bending from the hanging position the latissimus dorsi, primarily concerned in the effort to bring the humerus down to the side of the body, also indirectly

helps to depress the scapula and rotate it downward and to flex the elbow.  If the elbows are allowed to move forward the combined, oblique pull of the right and left muscles will tend to draw the lower middle back forward and to round the upper back. Similarly, the two great pectorals in their effort to draw the arms forward across the chest will also, unless resisted by the upper back muscles, cause a forward displacement of the shoulder girdle and flex the thoracic spine.  The contraction of such muscles, therefore, leads to distribution rather than localization of movement.

Gravity is another important factor in the tendency to distribute movement.  With every movement the center of gravity for the body as a whole is displaced more or less, or the centers for different parts or regions change their relations to the general center.  For every movement of one part of the body away from the general weight line in one direction, there must be a corresponding displacement of another part in the opposite direction in order to keep the general center of gravity directly over the point of support and so preserve the equilibrium.  The farther any part is projected beyond the point of support the greater is the tendency for all the segments between this point and the point of farthest projection to change their relative positions— to topple over or collapse.  The extent of this is limited by passive tension on muscles in a state of tonic contraction of varying degree, and finally by ligaments.  Bowing and stooping down with bent back are typical examples of movements produced by gravity and involving all joints from the hips up.

The degree of localization or distribution of a movement is often influenced by inertia, momentum and the recoil of tissues which have been subjected to strong tension.  This is especially apt to be the case in movements of considerable speed.  For example, in a charge the trunk tends to arch backward during the first part and to bend forward at the end of the movement. In a quick arm flinging forward-upward the movement of the arm is communicated to the trunk, causing a backward bending in the lower part of the spine.  After the arms have reached the greatest possible elevation they are apt to drop forward again from the recoil of the muscles and fibrous structures in front of the shoulders.  To hold a sharply defined position reached by a quick movement therefore requires additional work of a static character on the part of the muscles which produce the movement.  The range and distribution of any movement whatever will then be determined on one hand by the extent to which one or all of the above factors operate, on the other by the extent to which these factors are neutralized through fixation of segments.

Aside from fixation by external forces, the range of movement as well as the number of segments involved is limited in two ways:

(1) By passive fixation. When the motor force cannot be very accurately localized—as in the case of movements produced by muscles running over several joints, or by associated action of many muscles running in the same general direction over a number of segments, or by gravity—all the segments on which the force acts will move at the points and in the directions of least resistance and until resistance which the motor force cannot overcome is encountered. Such resistance is offered in the first place by the passive tension of muscles in a state of ordinary tonic contraction and situated on the side opposite to that toward which movement is taking place; secondly by the tightening of ligaments and the locking or contact of bony processes. In this way movement of the different segments is successively retarded or checked, two or more segments are locked together and move as one, and the motor force is finally brought to bear exclusively on those segments whose joints possess the greatest freedom of motion. Examples of this kind of fixation are numerous in movements of the trunk, shoulder and hip regions. Bending forward from the hips without making any special effort to keep the back straight has already been given to illustrate the action of gravity. Here the flexion in the hip joint is supplemented by a forward movement of the head, shoulder girdle and upper spine, varying in amount according to the tone of the back muscles and the mobility of the spinal joints. Only at the very last is the movement localized entirely to the hip joints. In the shoulder joint localization through passive fixation occurs only, if at all, at the very beginning of slow and easy arm movements, or at the extreme end of such movements when quick or forcible, after the limits of motion in the joints of the shoulder girdle and upper spine have been reached.

Passive fixation is rarely, if ever, sufficient to localize movement in a way to insure definiteness. In fact, when such fixation is allowed to determine the character of movement, definiteness is usually conspicuous by its absence. It is the mode of fixation used in large, vague, distributed or oscillatory movements, often forming parts of reflex coördinations, in which there is little or no attempt to localize muscular contraction, and in which accurate adjustment to varying conditions is not a prominent element.

(2) By active fixation. This is the mode of fixation used in definite, localized movements. Here the effect of the motor force on the segments which it is desired to exclude from the movement is neutralized, and displacement of these segments checked or prevented, by active contraction, usually static, of muscles opposed to such displacements. In new or unfamiliar forms of

movement the first attempts to localize by this kind of fixation are apt to lead to excessive and too distributed action on the part of the fixator as well as the motor muscles. This is shown by stiffness and jerkiness, sometimes by slowness and limitation of range of the movement. But with practice the individual learns to balance and time the two kinds of muscular action better, to confine both to the smallest possible area and to guage the amount and speed of the effort so as to produce a smooth and precise movement. This is the usual process in learning movements requiring fine adjustment, speed and power, or balance and smooth· sequence, such as walking, dancing, fencing, gymnastic feats, etc.

In gymnastics active fixation is used to maintain correct posture of the head and trunk throughout all movements, to increase the power of localized muscular action everywhere and particularly in the upper back and abdominal regions. By giving exercises which demand complete, powerful and well-adjusted contraction of the muscles in these regions it is hoped to increase their tone and endurance as well as the ease or facility with which they can be brought into play without inducing too strong action on the part of their habitual associates—the lower back muscles and hip joint flexors respectively. On this depends their efficiency as supporting muscles of their respective regions.

5. · *The Supporting Function of Muscles.* The' majority of the muscles of the trunk and lower extremities may be said to have two functions. One is to move the bones to which they are attached, and may be called their active or motor function; the other is to retain these bones in their proper position. This might be called their passive or supporting function.· The skeleton is a column of superimposed segments, held together by ligaments and fibro-cartilages in such a way as to permit a varying amount of movement between these segments. Because of this mobility the column is unstable, cannot be balanced and kept erect without steadying or fixation by muscles. The habitual posture of any part of the column will depend, for one thing, on the efficiency of the muscles responsible for the support of this part. The efficiency of muscles as regards their active or motor function depends upon their strength and size; their efficiency as regards their supporting function depends upon their tone and endurance. —Muscular tone, tonicity or tonic contraction are terms used to denote the constant, moderate contraction of muscles. It determines their habitual length as well as their (apparent) consistency. It is a relative quality varying in individuals and in different parts of the body. It is not necessarily proportional to the actual strength, size or development of the muscles. Nor does work which is conducive to increase in size and strength necessarily increase relative tone. The kind of work best suited for

the improvement of the motor function of muscles involves complete contraction against considerable resistance, alternating with complete relaxation. For the improvement of their supporting function work requiring static contraction (complete or nearly so) for considerable periods of time, relieved by only partial relaxation, or by complete relaxation without tension, is probably most effective.

In gymnastics the work should be of a character tending to improve the functional efficiency of muscles both as organs of support and of motion. This applies especially to those regions in which the constant influences of daily life tend to disturb the proper anatomical relations and to reduce the scope and variety of the muscular action to a minimum. To this end the exercises should, so far as possible, reverse the habitual conditions of posture and movement in these regions. They should cultivate the mobility at the points and in the directions in which it tends to become limited, viz., extension in the upper spine and usually flexion in the lower; upward and backward movement of the head, neck and arms. They should call for frequent complete, vigorous and well localized contractions of the upper erector spinæ, posterior neck and scapular muscles, or of the abdominal muscles and hip joint extensors, and for moderate contraction of these muscles at all times, under a variety of conditions and increasing difficulties. The results of diligent practice of gymnastic exercises of this character will show themselves in increased tone, endurance, and power of localized muscular action, in higher ideals and improved habits of posture and movement.

LITERATURE.

Albert. Zur Mechanik des Schultergürtels. Wiener med. Jahrb. 1877, Heft. I.

Bancroft, J. H. Posture of School Children. 1913. Macmillan.

Bowen, W. P. Action of muscles. Michigan State Normal College, Ypsilanti, Mich.

Braune, W. und Fischer, O. Der Gang des Menschen. Abhandl. des math. phys. Klasse des königl. Sachs. Gesellsch. d. Wissensh. Band XXV., XXVI., XXVIII.

Bradford, E. H. Movement of the Front or the Foot in Walking. Journal of the Boston Society of Medical Sciences. III., 7, p. 205.

Bradford, E. H. Flexion or Bent Knee Marching. New York Medical Journal, January 27, 1900, p. 109.

Brevoor, C. E. On Muscular Movements and their Representation in the Central Nervous System. Croomian lectures, London, 1904. R. D. Adlard & Sons.

Busch. Ueber die Function des Serratus anticus major. Arch. f. klin. Chir. Band IV., 1863.

Carlet. Essai expérimental sur la locomotion humaine, étude de la marche. Annales des Sciences naturalles. V. Serie, Zoologie, 1872.

Cathcart. Movements of the Shoulder Girdle *I*nvolved in Those of the Arm and Trunk. Journal of Anatomy and Physiology, Vol. XV*III*., 1882.

Cleland. A Lecture on the Shoulder Girdle and Its Movements. Lancet, 1881.

Cleland. Notes on Raising the Arm. Journal of Anatomy and Physiology, Vol. XV*III*., 1882.

Demeny, G. Les bases scientifiques de l'éducation physique, pp. 109-125. Also the whole chapter *II*., (pp. 159-245) and especially 4: fixation de l'épaule.

Demeny, G. Mechanisme et éducation des mouvements. Félix Alcan, Paris, 1904.

Demeny, G. Precision in Physical Training. Popular Science Monthly, February, 1891.

Duchenne, G. B. Physiologie des mouvements. Paris, 1867. .

Wernicke. Physiologie der Bewegungen, von Duchenne, übersetzt aus dem Fransössichen. Cassel und Berlin, 1885.

Duchenne, G. B. De l'électrisation localisée. Paris, 1872.

Fick, A. Specialle Bevegungslehre. *H*andbuch der Physiologie. Leipzig. 1879.

Fuchs, R. Der Gang des Menschen. Biologisches Centralblatt, XXI., 22, p. 711.

Gaupp. *U*eber die Bewegungen des menschlichen Shultgergürtels. Centralblatt für Chirurgie. 1894, No. 34.

Goldthwaite, J. E. and Osgood, R. B. A Consideration of the Pelvic Articulations from an Anatomical, Pathological and Clinical Standpoint. Boston Medical and Surgical Journal, 1905. June and July, p. 534.

Gray. Textbook of Anatomy.

*H*oughton. Principles of Animal Mechanics. London, 1873. Longman's.

Langer, C. Die Bewegungen der Gliedermassen, in besondere der Arme. Weiner med. Wochenschrift. Jahrg. 9, 1859.

Levinsky. Der Mechanismus der Schultergürtelbewegungen. Arch. für Anat. und Physiol. Phys. Abteil. 1877.

Levinsky. *U*eber die Lähmung d. M. Serr. ant. maj. Virchow's Arch., Band LXXIV., 1878.

Lombard, W. P. The Action of Two-joint Muscles. American Physical Education Review, Vol. V*III*., pp. 141-145, 1903.

Lovett, R. W. The Mechanism of the Normal Spine and Its Relation to Scoliosis. Reprint from Boston Medical and Surgical Journal, September 28, 1905, pp. 349-358.

Lovett, R. W. Lateral Curvature of the Spine and Round Shoulders. Blakiston's Sons Co., Philadelphia, 1907.

von Meyer, *H*. Die Mechanik des menschlichen Ganges. Biologisches Centralblatt, Band I, 1881-1882.

von Meyer, *H*. Die Statik und Mechanik des menschlichen *K*nochengerüstes. Leipzig, 1873.

Marey, E. J. Animal Mechanism: Locomotion. (Translated.) *I*nternational Scientific Series. D. Appleton & Co., New York, 1887.

Marey, E. J. Movement. Translated by E. Pritchard. *I*nternational Scientific Series. D. Appleton & Co., New York, 1895.

Mollier, S. *U*eber die Statik und Mechanik des menschlichen Schultergürtels unter normalen und pathologischen Verhältnissen. (With full bibliography.) In Festschrift zum siebzigsten Geburtstag von C. von *K*upfer. Jena, 1899.

Staffel, Franz. Die menschlichen Haltungstüpen und ihre Beziehungen zu den Rückratverkümmungen. Wiesbaden. J. F. Bergman.

Steinhausen. Beiträge zur Lehre von dem Mechanismus der Bewegungen
  des Schultergürtels. Archiv fur Physiologie, 1899. Supplementband,
  p. 402.
Vierordt. Das Gehen des Meschen in gesunden und kranken Zuständen.
  Tübingen, 1881.
Weber, W. und Weber, E. Mechanik der menschlichen Gehwerkzeuge.
  Göttingen, 1839.
Winslow. Exposition anatomique de la structure du corps humain. Am-
  sterdam, 1743.

www.ingramcontent.com/pod-product-compliance
Lightning Source LLC
LaVergne TN
LVHW021322150726
843309LV00015B/1713